"Is there anything you don't know?" Sachi demanded

"Very little," Dominic said without compunction. "I make it my business to find out."

"You had absolutely no right to delve into my personal affairs!" she retaliated heatedly.

"Don't talk to me about rights, Sachi. Your position is extremely tenuous."

He sounded so calm, so unruffled, whereas inside she was a seething mass of anger. "My position," she declared furiously, "is absolutely no concern of yours."

"What if I intend to make it my concern?" The query was softly voiced, yet deadly. A frisson of fear started at the nape of her neck and slithered to the base of her spine....

"It's quite simple," he went on in a drawl. "I want you to live with me as my wife."

HELEN BIANCHIN, originally from New Zealand, met the man she would marry, on a tobacco farm in Australia. Danilo, an Italian immigrant, spoke little English. Helen's Italian was nil. But communicate they did, and within eight weeks Danilo found the words to ask Helen to marry him. With such romantic beginnings, it's a wonder that the author waited until after the birth of their third child to begin her prolific romance-writing career.

Books by Helen Bianchin

HARLEQUIN PRESENTS

HARLEQUIN ROMANCE

Don't miss any of our special offers. Write to us at the following address for information on our newest releases.

Harlequin Reader Service
P.O. Box 1397, Buffalo, NY 14240
Canadian address: P.O. Box 603,
Fort Erie, Ont. L2A 5X3

HELEN BIANCHIN

the tiger's lair

Harlequin Books

**TORONTO • NEW YORK • LONDON
AMSTERDAM • PARIS • SYDNEY • HAMBURG
STOCKHOLM • ATHENS • TOKYO • MILAN**

Harlequin Presents first edition August 1991
ISBN 0-373-11383-8

Original hardcover edition published in 1990
by Mills & Boon Limited

THE TIGER'S LAIR

CHAPTER ONE

SACHI replaced the receiver with a mild clatter, uncaring that the action aroused the attention of her fellow staff.

Damn! She felt on edge—jumpy, she amended ruefully. All because of a seemingly simple request by her employer to contact a new client. However, it was the client's name that had caused the tiny seed of doubt in her mind to grow out of all proportion, and the resulting uneasiness was playing havoc with her nervous system.

'You're experiencing some kind of problem, Miss Tarrant?'

To have her employer breathing down her neck was almost the last straw. 'Nothing I can't handle, Mr Poissant,' she responded evenly, and suffered his narrowed scrutiny.

'Have you managed to secure an appointment with Mr Preston?'

'Not yet, unfortunately. His secretary informs me that most of his working day is spent in court.'

Neat eyebrows rose a fraction. 'Need I remind you that Mr Preston is a very influential man?'

'Which is precisely why I think *you* should take the assignment,' Sachi ventured politely. 'Or, failing you, Henri. *I* am merely an employee, and barely qualified.'

Dark grey eyes pierced hers, brooding and faintly speculative in expression. 'Mr Preston specifically requested your services.'

It was obvious that André Poissant was clearly puzzled, and not unduly slighted that his considerable experience had been overlooked in favour of a young woman who had been in his employ for less than a year.

Poissant comprised the partnership of two brothers, André and Henri, and was recognised as being one of Brisbane's leading interior decorating firms, renowned for its classic and neo-classic design. They specialised in refurbishing large old homes, André utilising his indisputable eye for antiques, while Henri took care of soft furnishings.

Sachi, too, had a love of antiques, a flair that was instinctive rather than practised, and a knack of being able to assemble items together in a manner that portrayed graceful elegance.

'I consider Mr Preston's patronage to be of the utmost importance,' André Poissant emphasised. 'If it isn't possible to arrange an appointment during conventional business hours, then you must make yourself available at a time suitable to him. You will, of course, be recompensed. The man is a prominent barrister,' he continued in explanation. 'His schedule must be hectic.'

I know precisely who Dominic Preston is, Sachi acknowledged in bitter silence as the Frenchman turned and disappeared in the direction of his office. What's more, I suspect there's nothing coincidental in the timing of his consultation with the firm of Poissant—nor his insistence that it should be with *me*.

Damn. *Damn* him! Why did his image have to continually stalk her? After all these years she should have forgotten, surely?

She'd been so young—a *child*, when Dominic had begun working for her father. A college student, he had represented the culmination of all her childish fantasies as a mythical hero—so tall, so handsome. In the beginning, he was the older brother she'd always longed for; her friend, champion—a defender against her sister Simone. With the onset of her puberty, Dominic's presence had taken on a different context, and the various shadings of friendship had irretrievably changed. Then he had assumed the role of dream lover, colouring her thoughts and invading her sleep. She remembered wanting so desperately to be grown up, and in her innocent mind she'd foolishly placed him on an imaginary pedestal, unaware that idols inevitably possessed feet of clay. Even now, the memory remained etched in her mind of a bright summer's day when, home on vacation between school terms, she had sought the company of Simone, the elder by ten years, and discovered her sister and Dominic kissing in the rear of the garden shed. Totally shattered, she had turned and fled indoors to the sanctuary of her bedroom, where she'd wept until there were no tears left.

After that nothing was ever quite the same again, and in the years that followed there was periodic media attention to remind Sachi forcibly of Dominic's existence as a man who had tenaciously climbed the ladder to academic success, attained it, then begun another climb to achieve a position in one of the top legal firms in south-east Queensland, winning plaudits for his brilliant mind, incisive and often acerbic tongue both in and out of the courtroom, and earning him a reputation for being ruthlessly merciless with any adversary.

Now, at the age of thirty-seven, he was an immensely wealthy man, socially sought after, and high on the list of Australia's most eligible bachelors. His photograph appeared with consistent frequency in the society columns of numerous publications as he partnered one beautiful young woman after another to a variety of notable functions.

However, the most unforgivable of all Dominic's actions in Sachi's eyes was his purchase of her old family home.

The insistent burr of the telephone interrupted her reflection, and she reached for the receiver, her forehead creasing into a slight frown.

'Miss Tarrant? This is Nicole Wetherby, Mr Preston's secretary. Could you please let me have your home number? As Mr Preston will be in court all day tomorrow, it would be advantageous if an appointment could be arranged during the evening.'

Would it, indeed? 'I have an unlisted number,' Sachi explained with the utmost politeness. 'Perhaps I could call *him* at home?'

'Mr Preston's private line is also ex-directory.' There was a slight pause, then the feminine voice became mildly persuasive. 'I don't suppose in this instance you could make an exception?'

Sachi took a deep calming breath, ready to consign Dominic Preston to the nether regions of hell. 'There wouldn't be much point, Miss Wetherby,' she said with unintentional cynicism. 'I waitress six nights a week in a local restaurant, and don't finish until eleven.' She paused fractionally. 'Unacceptably late, I think you'll agree, to make contact.' Aware of just how desperately she needed her job with Poissant, she forced personalities aside sufficiently to suggest, 'Perhaps you could relay to Mr Preston that the first available time I can arrange a personal consultation outside conventional office hours is Saturday morning.' She replaced the receiver before the secretary had a chance to speak any further.

A quick glance at her watch revealed that it was almost four o'clock, and she pulled her sketchpad forward in a determined attempt to conclude her suggestions for another valued client—a bona fide one, who was not intent on anything other than decorating an additional wing of his already magnificent home.

Sachi worked diligently, noting fabric sample numbers in sequence, her choice of carpet, the texture and colour, wallpaper, light fittings, even the type of wall-switches preferred.

At five she closed her sketchpad and gathered all the samples together before reaching for her briefcase, checking off a mental list as she added the items she needed. If she re-set her alarm clock for an hour earlier in the morning she could devote time to noting her suggestions so the résumé would be available for André Poissant's approval the next day.

Emerging into the main showroom, Sachi made her way towards the front entrance, aware as she opened the thick glass door that the sky was a dark ominous grey with heavy banks of oppressive cloud moving swiftly in from the east.

'Goodnight,' she bade a fellow worker as they both left the building, and without a backward glance she walked quickly round the side of the building to the tenant car park where her small sedan stood ignominiously parked between two vehicles of superior style and model.

Home was a small flat in suburban St Lucia, and she reached it just as the heavens opened and changed intermittent drizzle, rolling thunder and dazzling flashes of lightning into an undisguised deluge.

An old Queenslander in style, the large, rambling wooden house had long since been converted into four flats, its wide verandas covered in to provide extra rooms.

Sachi drove into her allotted space at the rear of the grounds, then ran quickly up the steps, where she paused long enough to shake excess moisture from her clothes and hair, before crossing the wide arched porch to her flat.

Putting her key into the lock, she entered the small lounge and closed the door behind her, painfully aware of the comparison between this humble abode and the gracious residence that was now in Dominic Preston's possession.

Her eyes began to mist as she recalled a time when her family home had been listed as one of Brisbane's most elegant mansions. She could clearly remember servants, a full-time gardener; parties, she reflected as she quickly crossed to the small bathroom where she shed her clothes and stepped into the tiny shower cubicle.

The name Tarrant had been a sought-after inclusion on any socially prominent guest list. There was a chauffeur-driven Rolls at her mother's disposal, and her father had driven a racy Porsche. Simon Tarrant's daughters had owned wardrobes full of clothes and attended the most exclusive of private schools, enjoying annual holidays abroad at various European resorts.

Sachi's mother's death at a relatively young age had devastated her father, and a series of risky business deals coupled with bad judgement had seen a decline in the family fortunes. There was also the sadness of her young brother Sam's being diagnosed as having muscular dystrophy.

The parties had come to an abrupt halt, and gradually Sachi had noticed items missing from the house as paintings were sold, antiques, the Rolls; and the Porsche was replaced with an inexpensive sedan. The beautiful Oriental rugs that graced the floors disappeared one by one, and the gardener's services were reduced to one day a week. The servants were dismissed and replaced by a cleaning lady who came in twice a week, leaving Sachi at nineteen to cope with a hard-drinking gambler who bore little resemblance to her father, and a young brother whose crippling illness became progressively worse with every passing year.

Three years later her father was killed behind the wheel of a car, and she had discovered that their home was mortgaged to the hilt. To meet household expenses and Sam's increasing medical bills she had sold off all the remaining antiques and paintings, given up medical studies, and gone to work. For a further year she had struggled to provide daily care for Sam in a home she could no longer afford to keep. The bank foreclosed and the house went to auction, purchased by Dominic Preston for a figure marginally above its set reserve. The press had made much of it at the time. 'Wealthy barrister purchases Tarrant property', headlined the state's major newspapers, and the various journalists hadn't refrained from revealing what their diligent homework had uncovered ... That as a young man Dominic Preston had financed his way through college, university and law school by working at weekends and during vacations for the Tarrant family as their gardener's assistant.

Sachi's present position with Poissant resulted from an unexpected telephone call from André Poissant just prior to the auction enquiring if perchance she had any further items from her father's estate available for sale, and the resulting discussion had led to an offer of employment. After more than a year spent typing in an office, the increased salary was extremely helpful, although it had proved to be a mere drop in the ocean of debt incurred by the services of a daily nurse and the ever-increasing burden of Sam's medical expenses. Sadly, the pneumonia she had been warned to expect had ended his young life a few months after she joined the Poissant brothers' establishment.

A flash of lightning momentarily lit up the room, followed immediately by a deafening roll of thunder, and, impossibly cross with herself for lapsing into such introspection, Sachi completed her toilette, then smoothed on sheer black tights and changed into a pencil-slim black skirt and white blouse before deftly catching her damp hair into a careless knot on top of her head.

A quick glance in the mirror revealed a reed-slim girl of less than average height with pale skin and classic bone structure, wide-spaced hazel eyes, and hair that appeared darker than its natural shade of ash-blonde. Twenty-five going on thirty, she grimaced, pulling a wry face at her reflection before gathering up a lightweight raincoat and umbrella.

The restaurant was intimately small, and owned by an Italian family who managed to run it with extremely successful self-sufficiency. Mrs Patrullo cooked, aided by her daughter Teresa; Mr Patrullo welcomed the patrons and kept a close eye on everyone, while his son Tony acted as wine steward. It was only because Tony's wife was pregnant and unable to wait tables that they had sought to employ an outsider.

Sachi was extremely grateful that they had, for it was scarcely five minutes' drive from her flat and, although the restaurant was always busy, the Patrullo family were engagingly voluble and pleasant to work for.

Tonight was no different from any other evening, and the rain appeared to have little effect on the number of patrons occupying tables. Consequently Sachi scarcely had a minute to herself as she took orders and delivered them, a bright smile permanently in place as she moved quickly between one table and the next.

It was after nine before she had a chance to catch her breath and begin doing justice to the plate of minestrone Mrs Patrullo put aside for her in the kitchen. The soup was so thick with vegetables that it was a meal on its own, and Sachi savoured its succulent taste.

The Patrullo family weren't obliged to feed her, but they did, insisting she take time to eat and brushing aside any protest she made. After the first week she had simply given in, grateful that her already stretched budget had gained a slight leeway in that she no longer had to account for six evening meals a week. Not that she ate much, but being able to rely on one nourishing meal a day meant she could exist on cereal for breakfast and fruit for lunch.

'Two people have just come in,' Tony announced from the kitchen door, and Sachi stood up at once.

'No, stay there,' admonished Teresa swiftly changing her apron. 'Finish your soup. I'll take their order.'

Within a few minutes she was back, pad in hand, her brown eyes alive with speculative interest. 'In a word—*wow*! *He* looks as if he's just stepped off the television screen, and *she* could be a model out of *Elle* or *Vogue*.' Businesslike, she crossed to where her mother stood in front of the big industrial-size cooker and relayed the order. 'Give it five minutes, Tony is serving their aperitifs.' She spared a quick glance through the glass partition. 'Another party have just come in.'

'I'll go,' Sachi said at once, standing to her feet and reaching for the order pad with one hand while she smoothed her hair with the other.

Out of the kitchen, her eyes skimmed the room with practised ease, then came to an abrupt halt as they rested on the couple who had been the subject of Teresa's comment.

There was something terribly familiar about that masculine head, even from behind—the perfectly groomed dark hair, the broad shoulders beneath the cut of his suit jacket. An icy finger trailed the length of her spine. Impossible, she dismissed as she threaded her way between tables and greeted the new arrivals, drawing their attention to the blackboard specials before handing out copies of the menu. Ascertaining that they required wine, she signalled Tony before making her way back to the kitchen.

It was then she saw her worst fears confirmed. There was no mistaking that splendid sculptured profile, no reason for a second lingering glance to determine if she could have made an error. How could she, when every detail about him was etched in her brain with the permanence of engraved marble? The last time she had seen him was six months ago across an open grave at Sam's funeral service.

Dominic Preston.

His presence here tonight garnered speculative interest as to his identity, for there were very few men who possessed his aura of power—something that emanated from within, and had little to do with the outer trappings of fine cloth, hand-tooled shoe-leather and immaculate grooming. Even as a young student he had shown promise of the man he was today. The lean, muscular build was essentially athletic, his shoulders broad, combining a dramatic mesh of classic brilliance with inherent sensual sexuality. Dark brown slightly wavy hair offset a wide forehead, chiselled facial bone structure, piercing dark eyes possessed of an ability to sear the soul, and a generously curved mouth that alternately promised passion and pain. It all added up to far too much. *Much* too much for any one mortal.

Without doubt, Dominic and his beautiful blonde date looked totally out of place in this small family restaurant. They should be dining at any one of several exclusive expensive places around town where vintage wine started at a hundred dollars a bottle, Sachi determined as an agonised voice from within screamed in silent rejection.

Why? Why this deliberate intrusion in her life? Blind rage momentarily whitened her already pale features. Was it merely a subtle reminder as to how the tables of power had been turned, or was there a more sinister reason?

At that moment Dominic lifted his head slightly as if sensing her scrutiny. For one infinitesimal second Sachi's eyes blazed with dazzling golden fire as she became trapped in the sheer brilliance of his gaze, then she deliberately moved towards the table of newcomers who conferred with an exuberant effervescence before finally giving their order.

Back in the kitchen, she collected a tray containing Dominic's order and carried it out to where he and his glamorous companion were seated.

A humourless laugh rose and died in Sachi's throat at the bitter irony of the situation. Now *she* was placed in the position of serving him, whereas years ago *he* had served the Tarrant family!

'Sachi. How are you?'

The sound of Dominic's silk-smooth voice created havoc with her equilibrium, and it was a miracle she didn't displace the cutlery as she set down their plates.

'Fine, thank you,' Sachi managed politely, aware of the slight narrowing of the blonde's glittering blue eyes at his recognition of a mere waitress. 'If you'll excuse me, I have another table to serve.' She even managed to summon a faint warmth to her smile. 'I hope you enjoy your meal.'

It was a busy night, busier than usual, despite the rain, and in a way she was grateful, for it succeeded in keeping her occupied. There was no time to think as she concentrated on filling orders and clearing tables, conscious as she did so of being under almost constant veiled scrutiny, her every action observed. It was a wonder she didn't drop a tray, or at least tip over a glass.

Her nerves must be well insulated, Sachi decided as she fought a silent battle with her inner self, and won. Not by so much as a glance or a lift of her eyebrow did she allow Dominic Preston the satisfaction of seeing that his presence disturbed her, nor did she permit herself to ponder how he had discovered where she worked. She simply did her job, and did it well, leaving at the appointed time of eleven to drive home in the unabating, pouring rain, before falling bone-weary into bed.

When the alarm sounded long and loud close to Sachi's ear next morning she gave an audible groan and fumbled sleepily to switch it off.

There was one improvement on yesterday, she noted as she opened the bedroom curtains—it had stopped raining. Which meant the day would bring stultifying heat and high humidity—an unwelcome legacy of a sub-tropical summer climate.

An hour and a half later she shuffled the catalogue together with her notes into her briefcase, then headed into the bedroom to change ready for work.

The roads leading into the city were congested with traffic, making her progress painfully slow as vehicles banked up behind computer-controlled intersections, to such an extent that it often took two changes of lights before she was able to gain clear access and any measure of speed.

Consequently, it was after nine when she crossed the revered portals of Poissant and took a seat at her desk.

André was suitably appeased when she presented him with her list of selections from the catalogue, and she felt immensely gratified when he agreed with the notations she had made. Now all she had to do was complete the résumé of soft furnishings and present it to Henri, allow both brothers time to confer, then perhaps by Monday she could ring their client and arrange an appointment.

At midday Sachi put down her pencil, then collected her packed lunch and walked out into the sunshine. There was a tree-studded park nearby, and several people graced the park's grounds, some reading in solitude while others talked in groups or listened to music.

Half an hour later she made her way back, and within minutes of her reaching her desk Henri Poissant ambled out from his office.

'Miss Tarrant, I have just received a call from Dominic Preston—via his secretary—requesting you meet him at his home tomorrow morning. He suggests ten o'clock. Perhaps you could ring and confirm?'

Sachi made the call, aware that as much as she wanted to rage and scream against the unkindness of fate, neither the Poissant brothers nor Dominic Preston's secretary had anything to do with the angry bitterness seething beneath the surface of her control.

CHAPTER TWO

THE prestigious suburb of Hamilton lay on the northern side of the city, and Sachi carefully timed her arrival at Dominic Preston's residence for five minutes past ten. It was a slight indiscretion that could easily be explained as the result of negotiating heavy Saturday morning traffic, and as she turned into the familiar tree-lined street it was impossible to restrain a resurgence of poignant memories.

She knew every tree, every house, almost everyone who lived in each of these elegant homes. Just as she knew in intimate detail the property into whose wide, sweeping driveway she now turned.

The grounds had been restored to their former glory and were impeccably maintained, she saw as she brought her car to a halt outside the imposing front entrance. The gracious stand of three jacaranda trees looked magnificent, their spreading bowers heavy with purple flowers, and the stylishly designed rosebeds abounded in a glorious blend of creams, pinks and red. Everywhere she looked there were carefully tended shrubs, and the lawns were smooth and green, their edges clipped with professional precision.

The exterior of the grand old home had been freshly painted in dazzling white, its peaked roof cleaned of moss and scale so the clay tiles bore a weathered terracotta hue that stood out starkly against the azure-blue sky. Even the mullioned

19

leaded windows glistened with cleanliness, and there were new curtains veiling the glass.

It was exactly as she remembered it years ago when there had been an abundance of money and staff to ensure its upkeep.

Unbidden, her eyes slowly slid to the main entrance. Had the interior been similarly restored? Not entirely, it would seem, otherwise Poissant wouldn't have been consulted.

Unless... No, not even Dominic Preston would be sufficiently calculating to bring her here under such blatantly false pretences. Or would he?

Even as she pondered the possibility, the object of her darkest thoughts visualised before her eyes in human form, his tall powerful frame clothed in superbly cut hip-hugging black trousers and a white short-sleeved shirt.

Projecting a striking mesh of animalistic sensuality and compelling authority, his saturnine features were politely assembled to reveal a greeting, although the depths of his eyes were without expression, so dark they resembled polished onyx, and equally unfathomable.

Was this what he was like in a court of law? Implacable, emotionless, and totally lacking in pity with any adversary?

'Sachi.' His voice was deep and deceptively mild, yet for some reason it made all her fine body hairs stand up on end in reactionary self-defence.

Her eyes met his with steady regard, unblinking and resolute as she inclined her head. 'Dominic.'

For an instant his eyes slid over her cool white blouse, lingering on the thrust of her breasts, slipping to her small waist, the fatigue-styled pale olive cotton trousers, to her low-heeled sandal-clad feet, before slowly travelling up to rest on her scarlet-lipsticked mouth.

What could she say? The ball was in his court; let *him* begin the game, she decided fiercely.

Perhaps he glimpsed something of her resolve, for he turned slightly and indicated the front steps with a wide sweep of his arm.

'Shall we go inside?'

Without a word she followed him on to the wide tiled entrance, through the open heavy-panelled door into the magnificent foyer whose parquet floor had been lovingly restored. An exquisite Chinese silk rug covered the central area, exposing a border of highly polished wood, and gracious items of antique furniture were strategically placed for maximum effect. The walls bore ivory silk-finished paper, and were graced with original oil paintings.

Silently Sachi followed him into the lounge, the breath catching in her throat as she saw a similar restoration had been effected.

Whoever was responsible for the refurbishing had excellent taste, she conceded dully as she followed Dominic through each of the ground-floor rooms, and she paused as he began to ascend the wide sweeping staircase leading to the upper floor.

'Why consult Poissant, when you obviously have no need of their services?' she queried stiltedly, aware of a slow, burning anger that had surged into life with every room she had entered.

He turned and regarded her in silence for several heart-stopping seconds, and she was frighteningly aware of his height, the vague stalking quality apparent in his stance. 'Because I require a second opinion.'

'Why?' she demanded starkly, and glimpsed the slight narrowing of his eyes before he turned and made his way to the head of the staircase.

'Come and see.'

'I don't think I want to.'

'No? Not even out of a sense of curiosity?'

Her eyes flashed with ill-concealed temper, and pain. 'For what purpose? So that I can congratulate you on a job well done?' Her chin lifted fractionally. 'Sorry, Dominic, I don't think I'm that charitable!'

'It would be advisable to bury your pride. André and Henri Poissant won't be impressed if you return without my written request for an estimate.'

'On what? The house has obviously been completely redecorated.'

'With the exception of one room.'

She looked at him with disdain. 'The mind boggles to determine *which* room. An en suite, perhaps? A small guest bedroom?'

'If you don't come upstairs and confer with me, I'll lodge a complaint to the effect that you were impolite and totally uncooperative.'

Sachi shot him a baleful glare. 'You'd do that?'

'You doubt it?' His voice was as smooth as silk and infinitely dangerous.

She was in no position to thwart him. Her job, more pertinently the money it provided, was terribly important and something she dared not put at risk.

Placing a hand on the newel-post, she slowly climbed the stairs to examine in silence, at his direction, each of the five bedrooms and three bathrooms, before coming to a halt inside the master suite.

In stark comparison to the rest of the house, the room was completely empty, although the floors bore the patina of new varnish and the ceiling had been freshly plastered. The adjoining en suite was little more than a bare room, with the original plumbing fitments removed.

Sachi turned to look at Dominic, seeing nothing in his expression except bland inscrutability.

'I want you to decorate and furnish it.'

'Money, of course, is no object.' It was impossible to keep the cynicism out of her voice, and she didn't even try.

'None whatsoever,' he agreed drily.

'Naturally you'll have some ideas.' If she didn't adopt a businesslike approach, she'd never keep a rein on her temper.

'I'd prefer you to submit yours first.'

'Why? It would be much simpler if you were to give me some indication as to colours; the ambience you intend to create.'

One eyebrow lifted in a gesture of silent mockery. '*Ambience*, Sachi? This is the main bedroom. I want it to portray a certain——' He paused deliberately, and she concluded,

'Masculinity?'

'I was going to say—feminine touch. Something a wife would adore, yet a husband could feel comfortable in.'

She looked at him carefully, aware of the aura of strength, the indolent sophistication apparent. He was a man who had achieved a high level of success, and knew exactly who he was and where he was going. What was more, he had the wealth to indulge the most expensive taste in anything he chose to acquire. But it hadn't always been that way.

'In that case, perhaps I should consult with your fiancée?' He wasn't married. She was sure to have read or heard about it, if he had been. His very status in society ensured that such an event would be publicised.

'My—*fiancée*,' he stressed, 'has every reason to trust my judgement.'

Wise girl, Sachi determined wryly. Only a fool would oppose him. Pastels, she mused, walking round the room. Something cool and fresh. Already her mind was racing with ideas. She extracted her sketchpad and began noting her suggestions. 'The bathroom is large enough to take a spa-bath. Do you want one included?'

His nod of acquiescence was a token gesture, and she ran an experienced eye over both rooms, then studiously ignoring his presence, she wandered about the bedroom at will, pausing at the window to look out over the grounds to the magnificent vista beyond.

Sitting high atop one of the many hills surrounding Brisbane, the house had a view encompassing every aspect of the city and its numerous suburbs from each room in this gracious home. Mount Coot-Tha could be seen with remarkable clarity, its bush- and tree-clad slopes standing out dark green against the patchwork of differing coloured roof-tiled houses.

As a child, Sachi had loved this home with a passion that had never abated, and although part of her hated Dominic Preston for acquiring it, another part applauded his taste in opting for complete restoration and refurbishing. New owners of similar magnificent old homes bought them only to demolish or remove the original structure so that they could erect a modern edifice of steel, concrete and glass, with the result that, although awesomely expensive, such residences were totally incompatible with their surroundings.

Turning back from the window, Sachi looked across the room and met Dominic's gaze with fearless disregard. 'There is one suggestion I would like to make in connection with this suite. An improvement which I think would make it complete.'

One eyebrow rose in silent slanting query. 'And what is that?'

'The addition of an adjoining sitting-room. A private retreat where your wife could comfortably read, or write letters in the evening when you're occupied with work in the study.' Her voice assumed an enthusiastic tinge. 'All the downstairs rooms are large, even the informal sitting-room. The bedroom next to this would be ideal, and would involve only the minor structural change of a connecting door. Or, if you prefer, merely a wide aperture. Unless you envisage entertaining a host of visiting guests, the loss of one bedroom isn't going to present a problem.'

Dominic looked thoughtful as he thrust his hands into his trouser pockets. 'Present me with all the relevant costings, samples.' His eyes caught hers and held them captive.

Her stomach lurched, then completed a painful somersault. He seemed far too tall in comparison with her petite five foot two inches. Overpowering, she amended, and portraying a silent deadly strength that was vaguely frightening.

'Will there be someone here on Monday?' she queried with forced politeness. 'I'll need to get a carpentry estimate on the connecting door as well as the aperture.'

'I employ a married couple,' Dominic drawled. 'Janet Armitage cooks and cleans the house, and her husband Tom looks after the grounds. You'd better give me the name of your carpenter, and I'll tell them to expect a call.'

Sachi revealed the craftsman whom the Poissant brothers entrusted to complete any renovation work for their contracted clientele, then, replacing her sketchpad, she moved towards the door. 'As a matter of interest,' she queried idly, 'who was responsible for the restoration and refurbishing?'

'A close friend of mine from Sydney.' He mentioned the name of a firm which was highly reputable and well known. 'We go back a long way, and I knew he could be trusted to do exactly what I wanted.'

They were descending the staircase, and as she reached the bottom step she paused to turn and look at him. 'Yet you excluded the master bedroom and en suite. If you valued his work so highly, why not have him complete the house?'

'Because I wanted your viewpoint,' he said smoothly.

'As some form of diabolical revenge?' It hurt to say it, even now, and the slow anger that had been simmering away inside her for far too long erupted into fiery rage. 'Isn't it enough that you've bought the house, without forcing me to come back here?'

'Force?' His faint emphasis was deliberate, and she tossed her head, hostility emanating from every pore in her body.

'Oh, really, Dominic,' she dismissed with scathing intensity, 'what sort of fool do you take me for!'

He looked at her carefully, his expression chillingly inscrutable. 'What makes you think I consider you a fool?'

Haven't I suffered enough? she longed to scream. Years ago she wouldn't have thought he possessed a hurtful bone in his body. Simone at twenty had been blissfully smitten with him, while Sachi, ten years her sister's junior, had been too young for anything other than childish adoration. In those days Dominic had displayed no hardened exterior, no hint of ruthlessness. Merely a burning ambition to succeed.

'Put it down to my vivid imagination.' Her voice was dry, and the smile she proffered didn't reach her eyes. How could she lodge an accusation without first being totally sure of her facts?

With professional ease she brought the consultation to a close as she crossed the foyer and paused at the front door. 'I'll ensure that all the relevant costings and samples are available by Tuesday.'

'You can join me for dinner. Shall we say six?'

'I can't.' It gave her tremendous satisfaction to refuse. 'I work six evenings a week at the Patrullo restaurant.' Her eyes resumed a fiery sparkle. 'Surely your informant revealed that fact?'

Dominic's eyes narrowed. '*Informant*, Sachi? Are you making some kind of allegation?'

God, he was an arrogant devil! 'Now why should I do that?' she queried with contrived innocence.

'I imagine a professional consultation in my office Tuesday afternoon won't present a problem with Poissant?' His voice assumed a dry mocking tone. 'I'll have my secretary contact you on Monday morning with a suitable time.'

Sachi gave a brief nod, and without a backward glance she crossed the wide veranda and descended the steps, aware that he walked at her side and was obviously intent on seeing her to the car.

A splendid Alsatian came into view from the side of the house and sauntered to stand at Dominic's side.

'Sheikh,' said Dominic by way of introduction as he affectionately fondled the dog's ears.

She reached for the doorclasp at the same time Dominic did, and her hand flew back from the momentary contact with his as if she had been scorched by fire.

'*Au revoir,*' he drawled with thinly veiled mockery as she slid into the driver's seat, and she refrained from uttering so much as a word as she fitted the key into the ignition.

The engine fired at once, and Sachi gave a silent prayer in celestial thanks as she sent the small sedan down the driveway. Clear of the street, she felt the tension begin to ease, although she was supremely conscious of a whole host of memories that had risen damnably to the surface—images it would take years to erase.

At precisely four o'clock the following Tuesday afternoon Sachi slid into a taxi and instructed the driver to deliver her to a prestigious block of offices in the central city.

It was certainly an imposing structure, newly completed, and an architectural concession to all that was modern, she perceived as she alighted at the main entrance and paid the driver with funds Henri Poissant had handed her from petty cash.

Endless square metres of smoke-tinted glass covered the building's exterior, and the entrance foyer was tiled floor to ceiling with marble. Leasing fees just had to be prohibitive, she mused as the elevator ascended with swift electronic precision to the twentieth floor.

It was impossible to still the faint flutter of butterfly wings beating inside her stomach as she entered the carpeted foyer and gave her name to the exceptionally well-groomed young woman behind the reception desk.

'Mr Preston is in consultation with a client. If you'd care to take a seat, he shouldn't be long.' The practised smile was politely detached, and Sachi selected a single deep-seated leather chair into which she sank with ease.

How long was not long? Suitably ambiguous, it could be anything from two to ten minutes.

Attempting to fill in time, she flipped through one of several magazines stacked neatly on a nearby table. Expensive glossies, she noted, encompassing business, fashion, art and architecture. The office décor was superb, promoting just the right note of professional elegance in utilising smoke-grey carpet with black leather chairs, an original oil painting on one of the suede-papered walls. Traditionally modern, and entirely masculine.

Sachi glanced up as an exceptionally attractive young woman accompanied a client through the foyer to the elevator, returning minutes later to pause within touching distance.

'Miss Tarrant.' There appeared to be no doubt as to Sachi's identity. 'Would you care to follow me? Mr Preston will see you now.'

Sachi followed in the secretary's wake, aware that each step taken down the carpeted corridor seemed to accelerate her inner tension.

The announcement of her arrival was professionally delivered, and she moved into the room, aware of the almost silent click of the door as it closed behind her.

Dominic's office was large, much larger than she had expected, and she felt a chill shiver slither down the length of her spine as her eyes swept to his tall frame positioned indolently at ease in front of a wide expanse of floor-to-ceiling plate-glass.

He looked the epitome of male sophistication, attired in an impeccable three-piece grey suit, white shirt and sombre silk tie. The true professional, she accorded silently, at once aware of his strong, arresting features that were a composite of broad-chiselled bone structure and smooth skin; dark brown, almost black well-groomed hair, and wide-set, penetrating brown eyes.

'Take a seat, Sachi,' he bade her smoothly, and she moved to a nearby chair fashioned in soft black Swedish leather.

'I have everything you requested,' she began as she set her briefcase down on to the floor and extracted a slim folder. 'Obviously you'll require time to sift through it all, but I've listed my personal preferences.' Her résumé was concise, complete, and accurate. She had taken great pains with it, and even André and Henri Poissant had applauded her fine attention to detail.

'Would you like some coffee? A cold drink, perhaps?'

Sachi looked at him carefully, watching as he moved towards an executive desk and leaned against its edge, his tall well-built frame a potent virile force in a room cleverly designed to project its occupant as the central focal point.

Was his stance a deliberate attempt at intimidation? His expression was impossible to fathom, and she didn't even try as she met his gaze with equanimity.

'An iced mineral water, if you have it.' Her voice was polite as she attempted to dispel the absurd sensation that he was an animal of prey. It was crazy to feel so *threatened*, and she tried to convince herself that the vague stalking quality apparent in the depths of his eyes owed itself to nothing more than her vivid imagination.

Dominic turned slightly towards the desk and depressed a switch, then quietly instructed his secretary, Nicole, to bring in coffee and an iced mineral water.

'May I see the estimates?'

He indicated the folder Sachi had removed from her briefcase, and she handed it to him, watching as he placed it on his desk and began flipping through the carpenter's written quotes before examining the numerous sketches and samples she had included, as well as her own copious notes.

Nicole came into the office with a tray which she set down on an elegant credenza, then, sparing each of them a brief smile, she quietly left.

'Help yourself, Sachi,' Dominic instructed without looking up, and she did so, undecided whether or not to take one of half a dozen sandwiches gracing the plate. 'Eat. You look like a wraith.'

Anger reared up inside her, tingeing her voice with a degree of acerbity. 'I'm not hungry.' Pride prevented her from accepting anything other than a drink, and she resumed her seat, her back rigidly straight as she fearlessly met his dark gaze.

'I don't remember you being so foolishly stubborn,' he remarked with dangerous softness.

'You hardly knew me at all, and then only as a child,' she responded stiffly.

His eyes narrowed fractionally. 'I beg to differ.' His voice was velvet-encased steel, and caused the blood in her veins to chill as he pushed the résumé to one side. 'I distinctly recall clarifying the rudiments of mathematics, helping you with poetic prose and championing your decision to enter the field of medicine. We were friends.'

Were was the operative word! 'Simone was much closer to you in age.' Sachi watched beneath carefully guarded lashes for the slightest change in his expression, and saw not so much as a flickering shadow disturb his superb control.

'I understand that she lives in America, and is recently divorced,' Dominic related with dispassionate imperturbability.

'Yes,' she revealed cautiously, loath to admit how infrequently her sister maintained contact. Mostly it was confined to a few sparse lines on a Christmas card each year.

'Also, that your appeal to her for financial assistance was met with an adamant refusal,' he added drily, spearing her with an alert, compelling glance.

The colour fled from her face as the shock of his words registered, and she was momentarily locked into numbing silence. She had to remain calm. *Calm?* She felt as if she was teetering on the edge of a precipice!

'How could you possibly know that?' Sachi demanded, enraged, and when he didn't immediately answer she found herself qualifying defensively, 'Simone's divorce hasn't been settled yet.'

'As her husband suffered massive losses in the stock market crash,' Dominic said cynically, 'there's very little to settle.'

Her head jerked up in surprise, her pale features becoming positively white as she demanded in scandalised disbelief, 'You've *dared* to investigate Simone? *Me?*'

His eyes assumed the hue of polished onyx as he subjected her to a steady analytical appraisal.

'Your debts are considerable and sadly in arrears,' he revealed with deadly softness, and his features assumed a chilling sardonic hardness that was totally at variance with his voice. 'Your one major asset, apart from a few inherited sentimental mementoes, is an aged and mechanically unsound car, which even if sold will scarcely realise sufficient funds to keep the creditors at bay for long, and without a car you won't be able to work for the Patrullo family.'

Shocked silence momentarily robbed her of speech. 'Is there anything you don't know?' she demanded at last. The words sounded stilted, even to her own ears, and her throat seemed tight almost to the point of constriction.

'Very little,' he said without compunction, and of their own volition her fingers curled into her palms, making a tight fist until the skin over her knuckles showed white.

'Did you *have* to buy the house?' she queried with unaccustomed vehemence. 'Wouldn't another have suited you just as well?'

'The only other serious bidder at the auction had plans to demolish it,' he revealed ruthlessly.

'How could you know that?'

'I made it my business to find out.'

'Just as you've made it your business to determine every detail about my life?'

'Yes.'

'You had no right to delve into my personal affairs!' she retaliated heatedly.

'Don't talk to me about rights, Sachi. Your position is extremely tenuous.'

He sounded so calm, so damned *unruffled*, whereas inside she was a seething mass of anger. 'My position,' she pointed out furiously, 'is absolutely no concern of yours.'

'What if I intend making it my concern?' The query was softly voiced, yet deadly, and a *frisson* of fear manifested itself in the region of her nape and slithered down to the base of her spine.

'I wouldn't allow you to do that!'

'So certain I can't provide you with a solution?' His eyes narrowed at the fleeting changes in her expressive features.

'Such as?' she countered cynically, and sheer bravado was responsible for the words that followed. 'A long-term interest-free loan combined with some form of employment at triple my present salary?'

His eyes narrowed fractionally, never leaving hers for a second, and there was a mocking twist to his smile. 'Really, Sachi,' he chided with dangerous softness, 'I'm sure you're capable of working it out.'

Anger brought a rush of colour to her cheeks, and she stood to her feet, so totally incensed she could have struck him. 'I'm leaving. It might amuse you to play cat and mouse games, but *I* am on company time!'

'Sit down.'

'The *hell* I will!'

Her eyes warred openly with his, and for several heartstopping seconds Dominic didn't say a word, then he shifted slightly, moving with lithe pan-therish grace away from the edge of his desk as he shortened the distance between them.

'It's quite simple,' he drawled. 'I want you to to live with me as my wife.'

CHAPTER THREE

FOR a moment Sachi thought some fickle imp was playing havoc with her hearing. She could only look at Dominic in stricken silence, frighteningly aware that he appeared to have masterminded a diabolical scheme to emulate the lifestyle once enjoyed by her family, and *she* was the final piece in his stratagem.

'My dear Sachi, I'm not proposing we live in sin. I'm rather old-fashioned about the sanctity of marriage.'

It angered her unbearably to glimpse a degree of humour lurking in the depths of his eyes, and her own assumed the hue of glittering topaz as she saw the edges of his sensuously moulded mouth tilt with unconcealed mockery.

Without conscious thought her hand flew in a swift arc to connect painfully with the hard angle of his jaw.

He seemed to tower over her, and she felt suddenly afraid. Dear God, she'd never hit anyone in her life!

Somehow she forced herself to hold his gaze— no mean feat when every defensive instinct she possessed silently demanded an escape.

'I might have expected that response if I'd attempted to proposition you,' commented Dominic with dangerous silkiness, and she spluttered into furiously angry speech.

'Proposition—proposal. It makes no difference!' She wanted to physically hit out at him and everything he represented.

Perhaps he sensed her intention, for he caught hold of her wrists, imprisoning them with galling ease, and she twisted helplessly within his grasp.

'Let me go, damn you!' Without thinking, she kicked him, achieving a measure of satisfaction when the pointed toe of her high-heeled shoe connected with his shin.

A second later she cried out as he dragged her close, and she struggled fiercely, powerless beneath his superior strength. She watched in mesmerised fascination as, in seeming slow motion, his head descended to within touching distance of her own. Her lips parted instinctively, silently imploring him to stop.

Except that it was far too late, and her mute entreaty went unheeded as his mouth effected a bruising punishment, forcing her lips apart as he violated the soft inner tissue.

A despairing moan scorched her throat, unable to find voice as he initiated an almost brutal assault on her senses, and she became lost in a timeless void, hardly aware when his anger abated and was replaced with a gentler, more seductive exploration that wreaked havoc with her tortured emotions.

If he meant to teach her a lesson, he had succeeded, for nothing—*nothing* she had ever experienced had pillaged her defences to quite this extent.

When he finally released her she stepped swiftly away from him, conscious of every breath she took, and her eyes blazed with outrage beneath his impenetrable gaze, until after seemingly timeless seconds her eyelashes lowered, effectively veiling her expression.

'Employing Poissant was nothing more than a farce, was it?' she queried bitterly.

Dominic was so close she could sense the warmth of his body beneath its immaculate suiting, perceive the faint exclusive aroma of his aftershave.

'Not entirely,' Dominic denied. 'I thought it only fair that my fiancée should choose the décor of her own bedroom.'

'I am *not* your fiancée, and I'm not going to marry you!' She was so furiously angry her whole body shook with it. 'I'd rather *starve*!'

'My dear Sachi, without my help you most certainly will.'

The truth of his words seared right through to her soul, annihilating her pride, her very existence. 'I refuse to accept anyone's charity!'

Silence greeted her outburst, a silence that grew incredibly heavy as the seconds ticked by, and she felt trapped, torn between the urge to escape and the need to stay.

'Especially mine,' Dominic acceded drily, his voice becoming silk-smooth as he ventured, 'Doesn't the opportunity of becoming mistress of your old home hold any appeal?' He paused fractionally before continuing with deadly cynicism, 'Your debts settled, a weekly allowance, and access to credit facilities giving you purchasing power with numerous stores and boutiques.'

He was a force unto himself; indomitable and obdurate. *Lethal.*

Her hazel eyes clouded as a hundred differing thoughts raced rapidly through her brain. 'You must be *mad* to think it would work!'

His mouth curved wryly. 'You think so? You've always loved the house, and approve the restoration I've effected.' Having placed the figurative nails in her coffin, he proceeded to hammer them home. 'Besides, we've known each other for years. The romantics will sigh over the alliance and become quite misty-eyed.'

An inner voice screamed in agonised rejection. 'I refuse to participate in something so deliberately calculating!' Her eyes widened infinitesimally, then warred openly with his own. For one wild moment she considered walking out of his office, and once on ground level hailing the first available taxi to take her back to Poissant.

'Why not see it as a solution to your financial problems?'

'Some solution!' she discounted vengefully. 'All I would be doing is jumping from the proverbial frying pan into the fire!'

There was a glimmer of amusement apparent in those dark brown eyes that made her want to pick up something and throw it at him.

'I'm not sure I approve the comparison,' he said with ill-concealed mockery, and Sachi drew a deep, calming breath.

'Approve or disapprove—I really don't care.' She turned and walked towards the door. 'I came here to deliver estimates and samples. I've done that, and now I intend to leave.' Pride kept her head high. 'If you choose to select any one of my submissions, you know where to contact me.'

'I require a definite answer.' The words were soft, yet beneath the silk was tensile steel.

Slowly she turned to face him, her hand on the doorknob. 'And if I refuse?'

For a brief second Sachi thought she glimpsed anger in the depths of his eyes, a momentary hardening, then it was gone.

'I will have no qualms about lodging a complaint with Poissant.'

There was a long silence, one that became increasingly difficult to break. 'Are you trying to threaten me with the possibility that you could use sufficient persuasion to terminate my employment?' Her voice was so deadly quiet, it registered as scarcely more than a whisper in the stillness of the room.

'You'd be unable to survive financially without it.'

'You're a barrister. Ethically, what you're proposing goes against everything that has to do with justice.'

'Do you intend consulting me in a professional capacity regarding the judicial system?' he drawled with hateful cynicism. 'I should warn you that I command a high fee.'

'What would you have me do, Dominic?' she demanded, hating him with all her soul. 'Concede defeat?'

'Would it be so difficult?' he countered drily, and she retaliated with incautious disregard,

'Somehow I don't see you as my knight in shining armour!'

His teeth gleamed white as his mouth parted in a humourless smile. 'Lucifer, perhaps?'

The devil? An involuntary shiver slid its way over her skin as she looked at him. As an opponent he was totally merciless. What would he be like in the role of husband?

'Why do *I* have to pay?' It was a cry wrenched up from the depths of her soul, and she was unprepared for the hand that captured her chin, tilting it so she had little choice but to look at him.

'You were a beautiful child, in mind and spirit. As a woman, you're irresistible. I've waited a long time for you to grow up, Sachi. *Years*. Watching, waiting for the time when there would be no one else for you to turn to—except *me*.' His eyes bored hers, his expression ruthlessly hard. 'I have a special licence, and a four o'clock appointment on Saturday with the minister of the local church.'

Sachi felt cold, almost chilled, and her lips were stiff as she vented her anger. 'You cold, calculating *bastard*!'

A muscle clenched at the edge of his jaw. 'Choose, Sachi.'

'I need time to think,' she stipulated with determination. Time, she added mentally, to come to terms with the possibility of living once again in the beautiful home that was now *his*. A wry laugh rose and died in her throat. It wasn't the *house* that posed the problem!

Dominic crossed to the desk, tore off a slip of paper from a pad, extracted a pen and wrote down a series of digits before handing it to her. 'My home phone number. Ring me there tonight.'

She met his gaze, her eyes silently at war with his own. 'I'm due at the Patrullo restaurant at six, and I won't be home until almost midnight.'

'Tomorrow morning, before eight-thirty, Sachi,' he insisted silkily. 'I have to be in court at nine-fifteen.'

He was utterly ruthless, and Sachi doubted there was anyone alive who could penetrate that hard exterior unless he chose to allow the intrusion.

'You're despicable,' she choked. 'I hate you more than I've ever hated anyone in my entire life!'

'So hate me,' he declared imperturbably. 'I'm sure I'll survive.'

'I'm leaving—*now*. I can't bear to stay in the same room with you for a minute longer!'

'If you don't call me, Sachi,' he threatened silkily, 'you won't have a job after tomorrow.'

'May the devil take you all the way down to hell, Dominic. You surely deserve it!' She turned towards the door, hardly aware in her anger that he reached it before she did, or that Nicole escorted her out to the elevator lobby.

In a daze, she rode the electronic cubicle down to street level and joined a lengthy queue at the nearest taxi-rank. It was after five, and when she eventually managed to secure a taxi the traffic had become heavy and particularly slow-moving, leaving her little option on arrival at Poissant but to slip into her car and rejoin the metal river of vehicles attempting to ease their way out of the inner city.

Never before had the delay bothered her to quite this extent, and she found herself breathing deeply in an attempt to alleviate the stress-induced anxiety of knowing she wouldn't reach home in time to effect a quick change of clothes and report to the Patrullo restaurant by six o'clock.

Yet there was nothing she could do about it, and she fumed inwardly all the way to her flat, laying the blame squarely on Dominic Preston's indomitable head as she called Teresa and explained that she'd be late.

To make matters worse the restaurant was un-usually busy, and twice she mistook orders and de-livered them to the wrong table. As if that wasn't bad enough, she dropped a tray of dishes in the kitchen, cut her finger on a jagged piece of broken glass, and to further compound a totally chaotic day her car petered to a stop one kilometre away from home and absolutely refused to budge another inch, leaving her no other course but to lock it up and walk home. A measure that was infinitely unwise, but with neither a telephone box nor a taxi in sight she felt hesitant about approaching any one of several darkened houses along the dimly lit street.

One kilometre wasn't that great a distance, but it had to be the fastest kilometre she'd ever walked, and once safely inside her flat Sachi sank down into the nearest chair, too enervated to do anything for what seemed an age—until Dominic Preston's image rose damnably to the surface.

For the past seven hours she had been too busy, too mentally occupied to even think; able to push her own predicament and Dominic's proposition to the back of her mind. Now it emerged with damnable persistence, and she closed her eyes in an attempt to shut out the inevitability of making a decision.

Oh, God, what *choice* did she have? She'd juggled loans to pay outstanding bills for too long, the gap between medical fees actually liable and government-subsidised refunds eating an ever-widening hole into her paltry savings, until there were none at all. And because she had few tangible assets the bank refused to co-operate, citing her commitments as being too many to warrant them approving any further financial reshuffling. So she hadn't been able to pay a seemingly endless list that comprised medical fees, nursing fees, funeral expenses. The letters requesting settlement had begun with polite reminders, then transgressed to stiff formal demands, followed by collection agency missives and finally the threat of legal action. From the onset, her honest attempts at appeasement by apportioning the major part of her wages each week into instalments had been reluctantly accepted for a period of several months, but recently there had been demands to increase the payments—something that was impossible for her to do. As it was, her flat was little more than a bedsitter, and its rent was only marginally above the cost of lodgings. Jobs were difficult to get, and she doubted there were any within her scope at a wage higher than she received at Poissant. Her car was a necessity, for without it she couldn't travel six nights out of seven to work with the Patrullo family, and she had coaxed it along gently for months on just petrol, oil and water. Now, poor overworked machine that it was, verbal loving care was no longer sufficient, and the probability of having to incur a sizeable bill for mechanical repairs was the last straw on the proverbial camel's back.

There was no way she could carry on alone, that much was clear.

One alternative was to run—simply pack up and move to another city, assume anonymity with a change of name and hope to elude eventual discovery by her creditors. Another possibility was to seek legal advice and declare herself bankrupt. The third, and last, was to accept Dominic Preston's proposal.

To run away from responsibility, although tempting, went against her principles; and bankruptcy wasn't something she viewed with any favour.

Weariness seeped from every pore in her body as she roused herself sufficiently to discard her clothes and slip into bed.

There was only one logical choice. Whether it would be wise was something else. Even on the edge of blessed somnolence the wry thought occurred that *wisdom* had nothing whatsoever to do with it!

Sachi woke with a start, unsure precisely what had jolted her from the depths of sleep, and she lay still for a few seconds as she allowed her eyes to adjust to the light.

The *light*! It was far too bright. Damn—she couldn't have slept in, surely? Yet the sunshine filtering through the curtains provided its own answer, and her eyes flew to the bedside clock, a hollow groan emerging from her lips as she realised the extent of her lapse.

Eight-thirty! She had no car, the nearest bus stop was at least ten minutes' walk away, and she doubted she had sufficient money in her purse to cover a taxi fare.

The only thing she could do, she decided as she fled into the bathroom, was ring Poissant and explain her predicament.

Within twelve minutes she had showered, dressed, completed her make-up, and all that remained was the need to contact André, who, in a gesture of apparent benevolence, suggested she take the bus and declined her offer to make up the time by working through her lunch hour.

A glass of milk helped sustain her appetite, and it was nine o'clock when she let herself out of the flat; almost ten when she walked through the door of Poissant. In that time she had agonised over the implications involved in not being able to contact Dominic, and alternated between relief and despair at the delay in relaying her decision.

At least twice during the day she picked up the phone and dialled his office number, only to replace the receiver before the call could connect. By four o'clock she could stand the tension no longer, and was referred to Nicole, who told her pleasantly that Mr Preston was still in court and not expected back in the office until the following morning. With reluctance, Sachi gave her name and requested that Dominic be informed of her call.

With no car, and a garage estimate citing several hundred dollars to restore it to minimum road-worthiness, she had little option but to take a bus home and phone Mrs Patrullo, advising her that she would be late. Fortunately she could count on a small advance against her weekly wage to pay for a taxi home from the restaurant. Another midnight walk was out of the question.

A refreshing shower helped ease the tension of a fraught day capped with riding a capacity-filled bus in midsummer peak hour traffic, and after towelling herself dry she slipped into a silk robe before emerging into the bedroom to change.

A triple staccato knock momentarily stilled her actions, and fear clenched her stomach into a painful knot.

Who could it be at this hour? Another representative from a debt collection agency? She felt ill at the very thought, and hesitated for all of five seconds before she reluctantly crossed to the door.

With extreme care she slid the safety chain in place before cautiously enquiring, 'Who is it?'

'Dominic.'

Sachi didn't know whether to be relieved or dismayed, and her stomach muscles tightened even further as she freed the chain before attending to the lock.

He seemed to loom very large in the aperture, his tall frame vaguely threatening, and her eyes slid up to meet his, encountering an inscrutability that was distinctly unsettling.

'Aren't you going to ask me in?'

She was supremely conscious of her attire, and one hand slid to the lapels of her robe in a nervous protective gesture while the other fell to the fastened ties at her waist. 'How did you get my address?'

One eyebrow lifted slightly, and the corners of his mouth tugged his lips into a cynical smile. 'André Poissant. Nicole relayed your message when I checked with the office via the car-phone.'

'André? But he would never——'

'Reveal a confidence? My dear Sachi, your employer is aware that I intend you no harm.'

That was debatable, and rested entirely on specific interpretation! 'I'm already fifteen minutes late for the restaurant——'

'I'll drive you,' Dominic told her with studied indolence. 'Your car, I believe, is out of action.'

Sachi looked at him carefully, seeing the purposeful intent evident, and something else she was unable to define. To oppose him in a bid for independence would clearly be unwise. 'Thank you. I have to change. I won't be long.'

'You intend I should wait on the doorstep?'

A faint tinge of pink coloured her cheeks at his musing mockery, and she stood aside. 'No, of course not.' She was acutely conscious of her flat, and its sparse well-worn furniture.

Dominic stepped into the lounge, and the small room seemed suddenly overcrowded. She paused momentarily, unsure whether she should tell him of her decision now or leave it until they were in the car.

'Don't agonise, Sachi,' he drawled. 'A simple yes or no will do.'

'You read minds?' she queried seriously, then attempted to lighten the words with a smile and failed miserably.

'At the moment, yours is remarkably transparent.'

She opened her mouth to argue, then thought better of it. Character assessment was something in which he would excel, by virtue of his profession. Yet she'd spent years masking her feelings, becoming adept at closing the windows of her mind.

It wasn't easy to be brave in the face of his pitiless implacability, but she managed—just, even if her nerves were a quivering mess. 'I insist that you clarify precisely what you expect of me,' she stated valiantly.

'An iron-clad agreement before you figuratively burn all your bridges?' Amusement lurked in the depths of his eyes, and something else. Respect?

'Yes.' It was no time to be faint-hearted. 'You didn't fail to outline what I would gain from the relationship. It's only fair that I should be aware what *you* require.'

'A social hostess,' he drawled. 'And a willing partner in my bed.'

There was nothing Sachi could do to still the swift tide of pink that coloured her cheeks and she instinctively lowered her lashes in a gesture of protective defence against his intent gaze. She was conscious of the pulse at the base of her throat thudding loud in a quickened beat, and it took all her effort to retain her composure.

'I'd insist on retaining my position with Poissant.'

'You doubt that being my wife will be sufficiently challenging to warrant full-time dedication?'

How could she answer that? With considerable care, an inner voice cautioned. 'I enjoy working,' she defended. 'Besides, you employ staff to ensure the house is smoothly run.'

Dominic pushed one hand into one pocket of his immaculate trousers. 'You don't see yourself conducting a shopping expedition every second day, and lunching with the city's social élite?'

'No.' She'd worked too hard for too long to become a social butterfly.

'I'm sure the Poissant brothers could be persuaded to arrange a consultancy involving four of five hours a day.'

Sachi hesitated fractionally, then said slowly, 'In that case, I accept.' There, she'd actually said it, and the implication of her commitment was evident in her eyes, widening them into topaz pools as she looked at him with unblinking clarity.

Somehow she expected him to make some sort of comment, but he merely inclined his head. Almost, she thought wryly, as if her decision was a foregone conclusion and therefore warranted no verbal acknowledgment.

'The Patrullo family will have to be told that as from tonight you will no longer be in their employ,' he told her.

'They've been very good to me,' Sachi protested. 'I can't just walk out on them.'

'I'm sure they'll understand when I explain the circumstances,' Dominic returned smoothly, and she felt then a familiar surge of resentment.

'I'm quite capable of doing that myself.'

'Did I imply that you were not?' he queried silkily.

'And Poissant? Will you also tell André? Or perhaps you already have.' A slow-burning anger began deep inside, threatening to erupt. 'I'm not your wife yet!'

'Go and change, Sachi.'

The temptation to stay and argue was almost impossible to ignore, and her eyes clashed with his for a few immeasurable seconds before her lashes lowered, successfully veiling her expression. Without a word she turned and walked through to the bedroom, slipped into her clothes, brushed her hair, then applied moisturiser and lipstick before re-emerging into the lounge.

Dominic's car was parked out front on the street, a prestige top-of-the-range Mercedes in pale metallic silver, and Sachi slid into the front seat to wait in silence as he set the vehicle in motion.

Pondering precisely how and when to inform the Patrullo family of her plans proved a wasted effort, for the matter was taken out of her hands on arrival at the restaurant as Dominic smoothly effected his own introduction, then followed it with the news of their imminent marriage, which immediately sparked tears, hugs, and effusive congratulations.

Attempting to work was a non-event, for Sachi was seated with Dominic at one of the tables and a bottle of the very best wine in stock uncorked, their health and happiness honoured, joined by several bemused patrons who appeared delighted to participate in a celebration.

It was unthinkable to consider eating dinner anywhere else, and Sachi welcomed the bowl of delicious minestrone when it was served, aware that the small amount of wine she had sipped had gone straight to her head—to such an extent that she placed a hand over her glass when Dominic made to refill it.

'No?'

'Definitely,' Sachi refused, wondering whether her confused state of mind was entirely due to the alcohol or to the manner in which Dominic was assuming control over her life.

'Aren't there any questions you want to ask?'

She looked at him carefully, seeing the watchfulness apparent beneath the smiling façade, and despite the warmth of the summer evening she felt suddenly cold. 'At least ten,' she managed with a wry attempt at humour. 'But somehow I don't think now is the time or place.'

'A desire to preserve the illusion of romance?'

His smile held a tinge of mockery, and she pushed her empty plate to one side. 'Illusion, Dominic? I consider *farce* more appropriate.'

'You want to renege?'

His silky query sent a *frisson* of fear slithering across the surface of her skin, and only sheer willpower stopped her from visibly shivering. 'No,' she responded quietly, and managed to effect a warm smile as Teresa served their main course, which she merely picked at, managing to fork a few morsels into her mouth in the pretence of enjoyment before replacing her cutlery, her appetite gone.

'Dessert?'

Sachi shook her head in silent negation, and refused coffee, knowing the strong espresso brew would keep her awake.

'Shall we leave?' Dominic suggested, and she agreed, although when it came to taking her leave of the family she felt close to tears, for she had come to regard them as her friends.

In the car, she sat in silence, her mind whirling as the implications of her liaison with the man behind the wheel began to take effect. She felt on edge—nervous, she amended, as the large vehicle purred down her street and slid to a smooth halt outside the entrance to her flat.

There seemed no doubt that he would accompany her inside, and she merely led the way, unlocking the door and then switching on the light before turning towards him.

'I don't have any alcohol. Only coffee or tea.'

'Coffee,' Dominic concurred, looking perfectly at ease as she indicated a nearby chair.

'It's the instant decaffeinated variety,' Sachi felt bound to warn him, conscious of his dark, enigmatic gaze, and her eyes slid down to the lapel of his immaculate suit jacket.

'That's fine. Black, one sugar.'

The kitchen-cum-dining-room was very compact and situated immediately adjacent to the lounge, therefore affording her little privacy as she filled the electric kettle. When it was ready she set both cups down on to the coffee table that separated the two single chairs.

'I suggest you allow me to contact André Poissant and arrange for you to take the next week and a half off,' said Dominic suddenly.

The butterflies inside her stomach completed a series of somersaults. It was starting already, the calculated manipulation of her life. 'I'm sure I could tell him myself tomorrow morning.'

His gaze was direct. 'You'll need two days to be fitted for a wedding gown and select all the requisite accessories.'

There was no way she was prepared for any of this! 'I imagined the actual marriage ceremony would be a very quiet one with few people present,' she managed with extreme politeness, aware that a digression into anger would only bring retribution of a kind she would prefer to avoid.

'Despite guests being confined to family and close friends, I see no reason not to observe convention.'

'It hardly seems appropriate.' Her protest sounded stilted, even to her own ears.

'I consider that it is,' Dominic declared hardily, as if his decision negated any argument. 'While I phone André, you can pack.'

'Whatever for?'

'It will be much simpler if you move into the house where my housekeeper, Janet Armitage, will be on hand to provide any assistance you require.'

Dear heaven, he was arrogant! 'I'd rather stay here.'

'Why make things more difficult?' he voiced smoothly.

'Difficult?' Sachi's eyes flashed and assumed the hue of molten gold. 'You can't possibly expect me to fall in with every suggestion you make!'

'It's the house or a hotel, Sachi. Make up your mind.' His hard intent stare should have had her quivering in her shoes, but she was too angry to take any heed.

'I don't see the necessity for either, but if I *have* to choose—a hotel suite!'

'In that case, I'll book you into the Hilton. It's central.'

'As from tomorrow,' she insisted. 'I have to attend to the rent, notify the electricity department and request a meter reading, organise for the telephone to be disconnected——'

'All of which will be taken care of on your behalf,' Dominic declared silkily, and pride was responsible for the rigidity of her posture.

'I'll pay my own expenses.'

'Determined to fight me every inch of the way, Sachi?' He picked up his coffee and calmly drained half the cup's contents before replacing it on the saucer.

'I refuse to be reduced to a performing puppet!' she was stung into retorting.

Wry humour lurked beneath the surface of that dark brooding gaze, which only served to fuel her anger. 'My dear Sachi, I imagine our wedding will receive media attention.' He paused fractionally, then continued drily, 'With that in mind, I strongly advise you to select traditional bridal attire.'

'In that case, order whatever you consider suitable, then have your secretary despatch the gown to the hotel.' Caution tempered her voice and she watched as he finished his coffee, his outward calm a chilling reminder of the measure of his control.

With indolent ease he subjected her to a slow appraisal, visually assessing her vital statistics in a manner that brought a rush of colour to her cheeks.

'Nicole has excellent taste, and won't object to extending her secretarial duties to recommending a bridal boutique,' Dominic acceded with smooth detachment. 'She can arrange an appointment for tomorrow afternoon. I'll have her confirm with you around midday in your suite.'

Without Dominic's assistance she didn't stand a chance, so why was she reacting so badly?

'Perhaps it would be easier if I ring Nicole when I've settled in,' Sachi offered in an attempt at civility. 'A lot will depend on what time I can get away from Poissant.'

'I doubt there'll be any difficulty,' he returned, unfolding his length with fluid catlike grace. No, she thought with wry resignation. All it would take was a few phone calls for doors to open magically and the metaphorical red carpet to be laid down. Omnipotent wealth promoted an unassailable power of its own, soliciting in most instances an obsequious desire to please by a host of minions. After several years of financial hardship she should be grateful, and she was, she told herself fiercely. Except independence had bred an inherent determination for survival—*her own!*

'We'll discuss further details over dinner tomorrow evening,' Dominic declared as he moved towards the door. 'Shall we say six-thirty?'

Sachi gave a nod in silent acquiescence as she crossed to his side, relieved that he was going. She found his presence unsettling, and it didn't help to know that three days from now she would be his wife. A fact she preferred not to give too much thought.

'Try to get some sleep,' he advised, subjecting her to a narrowed gaze, and her eyes flared slightly in silent antipathy.

'I intend to,' she responded coolly, and glimpsed a tinge of sardonic cynicism evident in his expression as he opened the door and passed through its aperture. She watched his broad frame descend the steps until he disappeared out of sight into the night's darkness, then she locked up and sank into the nearest chair.

Sleep was the last thing on her mind—in fact, she doubted the kaleidoscopic images swirling inside her head would settle sufficiently to allow anything approaching restful somnolence, unless that state could be achieved through sheer exhaustion. Perhaps if she emptied her wardrobe into suitcases...

After two hours of diligent work she had packed all her personal possessions, a small carton of edibles was assembled ready to be dispensed in the morning to a neighbouring flat occupant, and as she crawled into bed she was weary beyond belief— a condition she welcomed as she slipped into a deep, heavy sleep from which she didn't awaken until the alarm sounded at seven.

CHAPTER FOUR

As Sachi predicted, her entrance into Dominic's life magically dispensed with both minor and major obstacles in that the Poissant brothers' expressed delight and a desire to fit in with any plans she chose to make was magnanimous to say the least.

The hotel suite was luxurious, and without doubt, ruinously expensive, while Nicole, who obviously valued her employment, proved an efficient companion, managing to provide just the right degree of assistance without permitting a lapse into friendship, yet projecting the appearance of genuine enthusiasm and possessed of a keen eye with regard to fashion.

When it came to quitting her flat, even the letting agents proved unusually understanding and waived rent in lieu of notice.

Yet another subtle reminder of the extent of Dominic's power, Sachi perceived as she showered in the suite's beautifully tiled bathroom.

Her toilette complete, she crossed into the bedroom and selected a suitable dress to wear to dinner. In aquamarine uncrushable silk, the colour heightened the fairness of her skin, accentuating her naturally blonde hair, while the cleverly cut style outlined her slender curves. Although not following the latest fashion trend, it bore an expensive label and she felt sufficiently confident in its ability to pass muster in any restaurant Dominic had chosen for them to dine.

At six-thirty she was ready, waiting in a state of half-hearted anticipation, aware that within mere minutes a brief knock would herald his arrival. Somehow she doubted that unpunctuality was one of his detractory traits.

Nothing prepared her for the sound of a key turning in the lock followed within seconds by his appearance in the lounge, and she experienced a surge of anger at his unmitigated invasion of her privacy. It lent a fiery sparkle to her green-gold eyes, and heightened the soft tinge of colour staining her cheekbones.

The fact that he recognised the cause and responded with a mocking lift of one well-shaped eyebrow didn't help in the least.

'I distinctly recollect stating six-thirty,' Dominic remarked with deceptive mildness as he closed the door behind him and moved across the room with indolent ease.

'I expected you to have the courtesy to knock!'

'Good heavens, Sachi—whatever for?'

Oh, he was too self-assured by far! 'I might not have been ready,' she flung incautiously.

'In which case I would have simply helped myself to a drink and admired the view.'

It depended which view he was referring to! If he considered he had the right of entry into the suite, what was to stop him walking straight into the bedroom? She could have been delayed, or simply deliberately perverse in a desire to keep him waiting. Either way, he could have surprised her in a state of undress—something which she would have found embarrassing, not to mention unsettling.

'Of the city,' Dominic added sardonically, watching the play of emotions flitting across her expressive features.

God, he had only been in her presence a few minutes and already they were at daggers drawn! No matter how she felt, it might be prudent to attempt to defuse the situation. Resorting to anger would achieve absolutely nothing, except to highlight her acute sensitivity and merely provide him with a source of amusement.

Summoning a faint shrug, she held his gaze and offered without any conciliation, 'As you're paying for the suite, I guess you have the right to possess a key.'

'Limited access?'

Sachi's chin lifted fractionally, although her eyes became clouded with shadows and her lashes automatically lowered in protective self-defence. 'Forty-eight hours, Dominic,' she reminded him coolly. 'I'm sure you can be relied upon to impose some form of self-control until *after* the wedding ceremony!'

He was standing much too close for comfort, and she was suddenly aware of her isolation, the ease with which he could overcome any resistance she might provide.

'Afraid, Sachi?'

The soft taunt angered her unbearably, and her eyes flew wide with a brilliant flaring of molten gold fire. Pride alone was responsible for her stance. 'I've known you for years, remember? I doubt if you've acquired the need to exert force in order to gain a woman's favour.'

A gleam of amusement lit his dark eyes, and his mouth curved into a humorous smile. 'Preferring instead to indulge in the gentle art of seduction?'

Gentle? What was gentle about a tiger? For it was that jungle animal he most resembled! Strong, powerful, and utterly ruthless, portraying dynamic energy beneath an air of leashed control. A composite that was intensely arresting—essentially dangerous to any woman's peace of mind, she added silently.

As to being afraid of him? A hollow laugh rose and died in her throat. Any element of fear had to be based on her own response to his vibrant brand of sexuality.

'I imagine that's something I'll discover before too long.'

'In the meantime, perhaps we could settle on a venue for dinner,' Dominic drawled imperturbably.

Food had been furthest from her mind, but now that he mentioned it she *was* hungry. Come to think of it, she'd eaten a banana for breakfast, skipped lunch, and shared a coffee mid-afternoon with Nicole—squeezing that particular fortification in between necessary consultations and fittings for a bridal gown and all the required accessories.

'You mean you haven't already booked a table somewhere?' Sachi arched a delicate, finely shaped eyebrow and glimpsed his faint amusement.

'Would you believe I considered you might prefer to dine *à deux* rather than venture into a crowded restaurant?'

'Here?' she countered, trying her best to mask vague uncertainty.

'Room service provide an impeccable menu,' he told her smoothly. 'However, there are a number of excellent restaurants within the hotel. All it requires is a phone call to confirm.'

'A restaurant,' Sachi decided after a moment's hesitation.

'Safety in numbers?'

She ignored the quizzical gleam in his eyes, and crossed to the small bar-fridge. 'I'm going to have a glass of mineral water. Can I get you something?'

'The same.'

'Really?' She tried not to sound surprised, and glimpsed his smile.

'I'd prefer to conserve my palate for the celebratory champagne.'

'Dom Perignon, of course.'

'Or Bollinger, Moët et Chandon, Cristal—whichever you prefer.'

'What if I said——' Sachi paused as she handed him a chilled glass of mineral water '—a carafe of the hotel house wine?'

His eyes openly mocked hers as he gave a slight negative shake of his head. 'Unthinkable.' Without removing his gaze, he put his glass down on to a nearby table, then slipped his hand into the inside pocket of his suit jacket to withdraw a ring whose prismatic facets reflected the sheer brilliance of diamonds. She felt her eyes widen, then transfix with mesmeric fascination as he captured her left hand and slid the ring into place.

Diamond, Sachi amended, mere seconds later. An exquisitely cut solitaire in a simple setting designed to reflect its magnificence. Even as she admired its beauty, she was aware that it merely represented a visible symbol of Dominic's intended ownership.

'It's exquisite,' she complimented quietly.

'I'm pleased you approve.'

His faint cynicism stung, and she felt a tinge of pink stain her cheeks. What did he expect? That she should throw herself into his arms and thank him? If she did, it would be a false, gratuitous act— one that he couldn't fail to be aware of, and, no matter what part she might have to enact in public, her own innate pride forbade complicity when they were alone.

'I shall take great care of it,' Sachi managed evenly, momentarily curious in her subconscious mind as to how he had ensured the ring's perfect fit.

'Very well fended,' Dominic accorded with a twisted smile as he crossed to an elegant console and pressed the requisite digits. 'I'll book a table.'

It seemed so long since she had dined in such sartorial splendour that the luxury of her surroundings left her feeling slightly bemused, and despite the choice of dishes she ordered *soupe du jour* as a starter, followed by steak Diane with a serving of vegetables, and settled on a fruit compôte for dessert.

As she sipped champagne from an elegant crystal flute she let her eyes wander idly around the beautifully appointed room before allowing them to slide back to the man seated opposite.

To discover she was the subject of his attention was disconcerting, and she met his dark, enigmatic gaze with solemnity.

'How was your day?' Dominic queried in a light, mocking tone.

He looked so comfortably at ease, so relaxed, that Sachi had the most absurd desire to ruffle his calm exterior. 'Did Nicole fail to relay a suitable report, or are you merely attempting conversation?'

'What would you suggest, Sachi? That we opt for a mutual silence?'

His amusement rankled, and she set down her glass with care. 'I'm sure you're aware of Nicole's superb efficiency. Her devotion to you goes far beyond the call of duty. Consequently, her assistance proved invaluable, and you can be confidently assured I shall arrive suitably attired at the church.' She held his gaze without blinking. 'Henri and André didn't bat so much as an eyelid, and willingly stressed that I'm free to resume work whenever I choose. Even the letting agency was uncommonly obliging, and I can only assume such unexpected benevolence is entirely due to your influence.'

A gleam of humour lit his dark eyes, deepening the lines radiating from each corner. 'You could at least thank me.'

'Oh, I do. With the utmost sincerity,' she accorded steadily. 'If I'd had to manage quitting my flat and arranging time off from work without your help, I have no doubt that I would have been faced with quite different reactions from those I received.'

For a moment he chose not to comment, and the ensuing silence played havoc with her nerves. She had to be mad to consider conducting a verbal fencing match with a man who had won plaudits from his peers and associates for his ability to assemble the English language to its best advantage both in and out of the courtroom.

'Have some more champagne, Sachi,' Dominic drawled. 'This is meant to be a celebration.'

Dared she? Already she felt faintly light-headed, despite having progressed through the starter and the main course. 'Just a little.' She watched as he topped up her glass, and wondered if she could manage to drink it all. Surely he had to be aware that alcohol in any form wasn't her usual beverage?

'Tell me about *your* day.' The words fell from her lips without conscious thought, and she felt her eyes widen in slight surprise, aware that it had never even crossed her mind to express an interest in his work.

'Do you really want to know?'

Strangely, she had expected cynicism, but if it was intended she failed to detect it in his voice or his expression. 'Yes,' she said simply. 'Behind the sheer volume of necessary paperwork, there must be some highlights in the representation of clients. Courtroom scenes depicted on television usually appear so——' she paused, searching for the right word '—theatrical.'

Dominic lifted his glass and savoured a small quantity of champagne before replacing it on the table. 'What you see on screen is often an accurate portrayal, except that the reality is unrehearsed, pedantic on frequent occasions, often wearisome and at times immensely frustrating. It can also verge on the volatile. Justice must be seen to be done, although sadly there are times when misrepresentation contributes towards a miscarriage of what the judicial system is meant to exemplify.'

'It must be very difficult to exert enthusiasm for any client with a criminal record.'

ortunately I'm in a position to be selective. ugh, no matter how definitive the pros- n and defence, the ultimate decision rests with the jury,' he reminded her, and Sachi shivered faintly, aware that a bizarre twist of fate and circumstantial evidence could purport an innocent to be guilty.

'It sounds a fascinating profession,' she offered, and glimpsed a certain wryness in the musing twist of his lips.

'One I've always wanted to pursue.'

Sachi spooned a few segments of fruit from her plate, hardly noticing the delicious tangy flavour of rock melon and passionfruit, strawberry and peach as she reflected that after tonight she would be thrust into the limelight surrounding Dominic's life and forced to share it. A tiny shiver feathered across the surface of her skin, and she replaced the spoon, her appetite gone.

'What happens next, Dominic?'

'I imagine we complete our meal, finish the champagne, enjoy a leisurely coffee, then return to your suite.'

He was being facetious, and she experienced a renewed sense of helpless anger that she was merely a pawn and he the master player in this abominable situation.

'You know very well that wasn't what I was referring to,' she declared, endeavouring to remain calm.

'At a guess, the rundown to our wedding?' he hazarded with marked indolence.

'What else?'

'Nicole will meet you in the hotel foyer at nine tomorrow morning. There are still a few items to be purchased, I believe.'

'Good heavens, I can't imagine *what*!' Sachi exclaimed. 'To my knowledge we completed everything that was necessary today.'

'Nicole has my instructions, so bear with it. By midday tomorrow, or soon after, you'll be able to call the next twenty-four hours your own.' Dominic's scrutiny was particularly direct, and she summoned up a sweet smile.

'After tonight, the next time we see each other will be in front of the altar?'

'Your bridal gown will be delivered at one-thirty on Saturday by the manageress of the boutique—who will remain to help you dress. A chauffeured limousine will collect you two hours later and transport you to the church.'

'My!' Sachi acknowledged fearlessly. 'You've thought of every little detail! One could almost be forgiven for thinking you've done this before.'

'Nicole has been invaluable in an advisory capacity,' Dominic drawled with a certain wryness.

'Of course.'

'Finish your champagne,' he bade her imperturbably. 'You look infinitely fragile and desperately in need of an early night.'

'That bad?' She was unable to resist the intended barb. 'I imagined I was holding up fairly well.'

Dominic put his napkin on the table. 'Cynicism doesn't become you.'

If she didn't resort to mockery she'd probably hit him! 'Forgive me, but I've had every reason to judge life from a jaundiced viewpoint.'

There was no visible change in his expression, except for the slight imperceptible lift of one eyebrow, then a crooked smile twitched the edges of his mouth. 'A crash course in early maturity?'

The truth of his words hurt, and it took considerable effort to give a slight negligent shrug. 'That's one way of describing it.'

As if he knew she found the memory unbearable, he indicated that they should leave. Almost like magic a waiter appeared out of nowhere with the bill, which Dominic settled, and Sachi found herself being led from the restaurant.

In the elevator she stood perfectly still, and when it drew to a smooth halt she preceded him into the hallway, too enervated to do anything other than walk at his side to her suite.

Once there, he inserted a key into the lock and opened the door, then pushed her gently inside.

'Goodnight, Dominic.' The words slipped easily from her tongue. 'Thank you for giving me such a perfectly exquisite ring, and providing gourmet sustenance and superb champagne.'

He shot her a glance that held a degree of lazy tolerance, and an imperceptible shiver slithered down the length of her spine.

'Spoken like a well-behaved child, Sachi! Sleep well,' he bade with gentle mockery, and she was totally unprepared as he leant forward and bestowed a brief hard kiss on her unsuspecting lips.

Her mouth parted to upbraid him as he straightened, but he was halfway out of the door before she had the opportunity to voice a single word.

Damn him. *Damn him!*

The curse remained unmuttered, although none the less vehement in intent, and after sliding the safety chain in place she turned and walked through to the bedroom, where she discarded clothes and underwear with unaccustomed carelessness before slipping wearily in between clean sheets covering the large king-size bed.

She felt strangely bereft and close to tears, the victim of a complexity of emotions too difficult to analyse.

CHAPTER FIVE

IT WAS without doubt a perfectly splendid wedding.

Everybody said so, and Sachi felt totally alien seated at Dominic's side in the secluded restaurant he had chosen for their reception venue. Guests were restricted to family, in the form of Dominic's twenty-four-year-old brother Brent, a few close friends and selected associates—all of them virtual strangers, for when asked she hadn't been able to think of a solitary person of consequence who merited an invitation.

The entire proceedings had assumed a quality of unreality from the moment when, hours earlier, she had been transformed into something resembling a combination of bridal model and fairy princess by a hairdresser, beautician and boutique manageress.

Like a mechanical doll, Sachi had walked down the aisle on Brent's arm, where at the altar she repeated prompted vows, exchanged rings, then stepped out into the summer sunshine as Mrs Sachi Alyse *Preston*.

Now, with strains of the bridal waltz being struck by the band quartet, she accepted Dominic's hand and moved with him towards the small dance-floor, all too aware that they were the focus of attention. It was years since she had last danced, and she felt incredibly nervous in case she missed her step.

To her husband's credit, she didn't, and in his arms she followed his experienced lead, feeling immensely grateful when their solitary circle was completed and they were joined by fellow guests.

Although seconds later Sachi wasn't so sure, for Dominic's arms had drawn her inextricably close—too close, she thought silently, aware with almost frightening clarity that soon they must leave the restaurant and their guests behind.

A tiny shiver whispered its way down the length of her spine, then slowly spread over the surface of her skin, lifting all her fine body hairs in a prickling gesture of self-defence.

'Cold?'

If she were to answer truthfully, she would have to say yes—but such a response was tantamount to an admission of sorts, and she refused to give him the satisfaction of knowing her nerves were slowly shredding into countless threads.

'No.' Even to her own ears her voice sounded impossibly husky and indistinct. Heavens, she'd have to try harder in her attempt to act out an expected part! Summoning all her resources, she offered quietly, 'You've gone to considerable trouble and expense to make today seem as realistic as possible.'

His warm breath teased the tendrils of hair at her temple, and she could sense the faint amusement apparent in his response.

'What did you expect—a civil ceremony conducted by a celebrant with the requisite two witnesses?'

Her features were pale and her beautiful green-gold eyes seemed absurdly large as she lifted her head and spared him a solemn glance. 'If you remember, I had no say in the matter.'

Incredibly, those shrewd, piercing brown eyes softened slightly, and devoid of their usual cynicism they became almost-sympathetic. 'Keep it up for a little longer, Sachi. You're doing fine.'

'Am I?' There was a strange sadness in her voice that she had no intention of allowing to emerge. 'I feel as if I'm floating, and all this is part of a dream.'

Even as she said the words she wondered if the dream might soon assume the proportions of a nightmare. Inevitably they would be alone, although where was a subject for conjecture—a hotel suite, perhaps? Surely not his elegant Hamilton residence? Somehow having to endure an introduction to sexual intimacies in her former family home seemed too much of a sacrilege.

'Did I tell you we're driving down to the Gold Coast tonight?'

Was mind-reading part of his repertoire? 'You know you didn't, she declared, forcing herself to hold his gaze—to smile, even if it was a shaky facsimile. 'For how long?'

'A few days.'

Her stomach lurched, nerves tautening in cataclysmic rejection so that she actually felt ill. Only an incredible feat of acting kept her smile in place, although her eyes were dark and totally devoid of expression.

Time held little significance after that, and she had no recollection whether it was one hour or two before she accompanied Dominic in the completion of a slow circle of the restaurant as they thanked and took leave of their guests.

A chauffeured limousine stood waiting at the door, and within minutes the driver eased the large vehicle away from the kerb into the flow of traffic.

Why did it always seem to take an age to reach a desired destination, yet an undesired one could be achieved in a very short space of time? Sachi wondered as the limousine swept to a halt outside the entrance to Dominic's elegant home.

Her home now. She should be happy to return. Even joyful, that so much cost and effort had gone into its restoration, for the end result was perfection. Yet all she could think of was the price she had to pay, and the man who would skilfully exact it.

If only it were tomorrow. At least then she wouldn't be a quivering emotional wreck! Take hold of yourself, she admonished silently as she slid out from the car. Eight hours from now, the night and all it held would be over.

'We'll get changed, then head down to the Coast,' Dominic told her smoothly after dismissing the limousine. 'The Hilton delivered your belongings here. I'm sure it won't take you long to pack.'

Sachi merely inclined her head in mute acquiescence, for her voice seemed locked in her throat, and she watched with detachment as he inserted a key into the front door.

'What do you think you're doing?' Sachi gasped in shocked disbelief seconds later as he swept her high into his arms.

'Observing tradition,' Dominic drawled.

'Put me down!'

His response was tinged with mocking cynicism. 'You're as light as a feather.'

'I'm quite capable of walking,' Sachi declared angrily.

'Did I suggest that you weren't?'

They'd only been married a few hours and already they were arguing! 'Please.' It wasn't an unequivocal capitulation, and after a few seconds he allowed her to slip down to her feet.

'Go upstairs and change,' he directed. 'We're using the guest-room until alterations to our own suite have been completed.'

Sachi's eyes widened slightly in surprise. 'You decided to go ahead with my suggestion to turn the adjacent bedroom into a private sitting-room?'

His eyes speared hers, enigmatic and faintly mocking. 'Have you changed your mind?'

'No, of course not.'

'Good. The workmen begin next week.'

Sachi couldn't think of a single thing to say, and in silence she turned and made for the stairs, supremely conscious of the man following close behind.

She felt physically and emotionally drained, ill at ease, and terribly on edge. It had been a long day, and all she really wanted to do was take a leisurely shower, then slip into bed. Alone.

Except that it would be at least two hours before she could do that, and she doubted that the invention of a mythical headache would fool Dominic in the slightest.

On reaching the upper floor she entered the guest-room, seeing at once evidence of Dominic's occupancy from the partly packed bag reposing on an elegantly upholstered stool, to the neat stack of folded clothes on the edge of the bed. A matching bag lay open nearby, together with a set of exquisite lingerie, various items of underwear, swimsuit and bikini, and a selection of skirts, blouses, dresses—all new, and obviously meant for her.

To think that he had authorised someone, presumably Nicole, to purchase them made her feel incredibly angry. 'My wardrobe is adequate,' she declared the instant he followed her into the room. 'And hardly of the Cinderella sackcloth variety.' Sweeping a hand towards the elegant pile of clothes, she turned to face him. 'I don't need these.'

'Nevertheless, you'll accept them,' Dominic stated firmly, and, reaching forward, he took hold of her chin, lifting it so she had no option but to look at him. 'Your eyes are wide and stormy,' he mused as he slowly raked her features. 'With dignity and pride masking an element of fear.'

Her eyes seemed to widen even further, and she looked at him with glittering anger. 'I'm not sure I want to be subjected to analysis.'

'Is that what I'm doing?' His thumb moved to the edge of her mouth, then slowly traced its sensitive lower curve.

A strange weakness invaded her limbs, and she blamed the champagne. 'I think you're cleverly attempting to undermine my resistance.'

His soft chuckle set the butterflies in her stomach fluttering into life, and she placed her hands on his chest in an effort to push him away. Except that somehow her actions merely brought him closer, and she stood in rigid silence as he released her chin and carefully removed the pins holding her headdress in place. Then, before she could stop him, he turned her round and began undoing the long line of button-loops stretching from just below her nape to the base of her spine.

'You should be able to manage the rest on your own.'

God, he was so—*imperturbable*! Almost as if he had completed this simple personal chore a hundred times before. That he undoubtedly had merely threw her tenuous emotions into further turmoil. Yet she was damned if she would permit herself to be shaken by it.

'Thank you,' she managed calmly, turning away from him. Somehow she had to effect a change of clothes in his presence without giving any outward sign of embarrassment.

Don't think, just do it, an inner voice bade, and with slightly shaky fingers she undid the remaining loops, untied the hooped underslip, then stepped carefully out of the gown. Attired in a white teddy and sheer white stockings held up by a lacy suspender-belt, she was adequately covered, but it took considerable effort to walk casually across to the wardrobe and select a suitable dress. Even more courage to calmly meet his eyes as he moved to within touching distance and unhurriedly selected trousers and a shirt from the adjoining robe space.

Sachi wanted to scream that it wasn't fair—that Dominic could have permitted her some privacy. Except that the words never found voice, and she successfully masked her resentment as she slipped the dress over her head, then slid the zip fastener closed.

Within a matter of minutes she had carefully put her wedding gown on a hanger and completed her packing.

'Ready?'

She doubted it would make any difference if she answered no—except make an extremely provocative situation even more difficult. ''Yes.'

His eyes speared hers, dark and unfathomable, and she felt her own widen in silent self-preservation. 'You hardly ate a thing at the reception. Would you like some coffee, a sandwich, before we leave?'

She hesitated, unsure whether food would further unsettle the nerves in her stomach, and hedged lightly, 'Hadn't we better get on our way? It will be after midnight before we reach the hotel.'

'We're staying at Bayview Harbour. I own an apartment in the Les Colonnades tower.'

Sachi's heart seemed to thud unevenly beneath her breast. 'Of course,' she said with a faint smile. 'I should have known you'd be sufficiently far-sighted to invest in property on the Gold Coast.'

Without a word Dominic collected a bag in each hand, then cast her a discerning look. 'I'll take these down to the car, then we'll have some coffee.'

And delay the inevitable? A silent scream rose up in her throat, then died before it could find voice. 'No, really. I'd rather wait until we get to the Coast.'

How could she tell him the past few days had been hell, a slow torture that had annihilated her very soul? The wedding ceremony had merely been a legal formality. Tonight was something else.

Dominic's eyes narrowed fractionally, then much to Sachi's relief he merely turned and walked from the room.

In the car she sat in silence, experiencing measurable relief when Dominic activated the car stereo system, and she simply leaned back against the headrest and viewed the passing illuminated night-time scenery.

As they progressed along the F3 the bright suburban lights began to merge into dark shadowy countryside. Sheer weariness and soft music combined to provide a state of lulled inertia, and after long, dragging minutes she simply gave up the fight against sleep and closed her eyes.

Sachi woke at the sound of her name, instantly alert after years of having Sam call out in the night, and for a few brief seconds she felt totally disorientated with her surroundings.

Then realisation dawned as she saw Dominic standing beside the open passenger door of the car, and her eyes assumed a haunted quality. 'We've arrived,' she said unnecessarily.

'Yes. I've already retrieved our bags from the boot.'

With slow, unhurried movements she undid her seatbelt and slid out from the car. The underground car park was well lit, and on entering the elevator she stood in silence as it transferred them with swift electronic precision to the twelfth floor.

The apartment was tastefully modern, Sachi couldn't help noticing, utilising a pleasing blend of colours designed to accentuate space and light. Pale silver-grey carpets were complemented by deep purple-amethyst leather sofas in the lounge, a glass-topped table and mushroom lacquered chairs in the dining-room. 'It's beautiful,' she accorded simply.

Dominic's expression was impossible to gauge as he turned slightly to face her, and her eyes slid away to a point just above his right shoulder.

'Thank you. I'll take our bags through to the bedroom.'

That last word seemed to reverberate through her brain, and in an effort to retain a semblance of calm she inclined her head. 'I'll come with you, then I can unpack and take a shower.'

Her voice sounded normal, even to her own ears, and she wondered at her ability to project such a seemingly relaxed façade when inside she was a quivering mass of nerves.

'While I open the champagne?' Dominic drawled.

The thought of slipping into an alcoholic haze was infinitely tempting, except that she'd already sipped her way through almost two glasses this evening. Much more, and she'd probably be physically ill. 'I'd prefer coffee, if you don't mind.'

'I'll make it as soon as I've showered.'

The breath caught in her throat, and she was sure her eyes had become impossibly wide.

'There are two bathrooms,' he informed her with intended mockery. 'Although I'm not averse to sharing...' He trailed to a deliberate halt, then arched a quizzical eyebrow at her shocked expression. 'No?' His smile was entirely cynical. 'Not yet, perhaps.'

'Not ever!'

'My dear wife—so vehement? *Never* is a long time.'

Sachi was consumed by a mixture of emotions, the foremost being anger at his attempt to provoke, and she longed to lash out against him. Except caution tempered her response—that, and a desire not to sound like an outraged child.

'Why not show me the rest of the apartment?' Dammit, she was even able to match his cynicism, and she felt a small surge of victory.

'By all means,' he declared smoothly, touching light switches as he progressed through the hallway.

With considerable effort she managed to summon forth a measure of professional interest as he indicated the guest bedroom. The blend of amethyst, mushroom and two shades of palest pink had been utilised to advantage, with both bedheads and pedestals lacquered in amethyst and the soft furnishings reflecting muted tones.

However, in the main bedroom the colours had been reversed, with the bedspread and curtains in the dark purple of Oriental amethyst providing an excellent foil for pale mushroom lacquered bedhead and pedestals.

Sachi recognised the designer's imaginative flair and applauded the professional result that was neither too masculine nor too feminine, merely a pleasing combination of both.

'I'll unpack what I need,' Dominic drawled, and proceeded to unzip his bag, while she followed suit.

As he was about to leave the room she told him civilly, 'I like my coffee with a dash of milk, no sugar.'

'Percolated?'

'Decaffeinated, and preferably instant.'

His soft laugh almost succeeded in unnerving her, and her hands shook slightly as she completed her unpacking.

Nicole's extensive shopping list had included elegant lingerie, and Sachi simply reached for a beautiful nightgown and matching wrap in lace-edged soft cream satin before moving into the adjoining en suite.

After removing her make-up, she pinned up her hair, then turned on the taps and stepped into the shower cubicle to emerge several minutes later feeling refreshed, then, towelled dry and her toilette complete, she donned the nightgown and quickly slid her arms into the matching wrap. A quick application of the brush and her hair was restored to order, although instead of leaving it loose she opted to twist it into one long plait.

Without being consciously aware of doing so, she examined her reflected image with a certain amount of detachment, viewing the fine-boned facial features as if they belonged to someone else. Free of make-up she looked younger than her twenty-five years, although on closer inspection her eyes appeared incredibly solemn and far too large. There was also some vital element missing, and after a few soul-searching seconds she realised sadly that it was *joie de vivre*.

With a mental shake she decided that such introspection was detrimental, for it merely undermined self-assurance and bred anxiety. Which hardly made sense, for she had weathered so much in the past, and managed, hadn't she? Dealt with taciturn unhelpful bank managers, irate landlords and menacing creditors. By sheer courage and tenacity, she had become a survivor. Marriage to Dominic Preston might be akin to bearding a figurative tiger in his lair, but she had entered into it with her eyes open and now was not the time to be faint-hearted!

Emerging from the en suite, she crossed the bedroom and moved down the hallway towards the lounge, inwardly determined to project a mature façade.

Which worked perfectly well until she saw Dominic standing indolently at ease in the middle of the room. Seeing him attired in a white towelling robe which emphasised the steel-muscled strength of his indecently broad shoulders, it didn't take much imagination to realise how he would look unadorned, Sachi thought wildly, and felt her pulse trip its beat and leap into quickened life as she moved towards him.

With concentrated effort she forced herself to meet the steadiness of those dark enigmatic eyes.

'I've fixed a snack, and the kettle is hot.'

If she ate anything, her stomach would immediately revolt! Oh, God, she pleaded silently, was there no easy way out of this? 'I'll just have coffee,' she told him.

His eyes narrowed fractionally. 'You look pale—and incredibly fragile.'

'I'm really very resilient.' She sounded so calm, it was almost amusing, and a bubble of hysterical laughter rose and died in her throat. With a sense of desperation she moved towards the kitchen where she poured water into both cups with care, glad that her body shielded the slight shakiness of her hands as she fetched milk from the refrigerator.

'I have a boat moored at the marina,' Dominic drawled after taking an appreciative mouthful of coffee. 'How do you feel about taking a cruise up to Sanctuary Cove tomorrow?'

'That sounds fine,' she acknowledged carefully.

'My dear Sachi,' he mocked, 'from the tone of your voice, you're treading on eggshells. Why?'

'Because very soon I'm going to have to share your bed.'

'Ah, *honesty*. How commendable!'

He was amused, damn him! Her knuckles showed white as she clenched the handle of her cup, and a defiant sparkle lent her eyes the brilliance of diamond-cut topaz. 'It's my only defence.'

His expression assumed a wary stillness. 'I'm not your executioner.'

'Aren't you?'

Sachi watched as he drained his cup and placed it on the sink-bench. For some inexplicable reason she couldn't breathe, and her heart assumed a rapid beat as his eyes raked her pale features.

'Go to bed. It's been a long day.'

Her nerves felt as if they were stretched to breaking point. 'Oh, stop treating me like a child!'

Dominic reached out and caught hold of her chin, lifting it slightly despite her effort to resist. 'I doubt if you're ready to be treated as a woman.'

'What makes you so sure?'

'Quit while you're ahead, Sachi.'

The deadly softness in his voice sent shivers scudding down the length of her spine, and she made no protest as he removed the cup from her nerveless fingers.

With indolent litheness he moved towards the door, his tall frame seeming to fill the aperture as he paused to bid her goodnight.

She watched in mesmerised fascination as he disappeared down the hallway. Her lips parted in surprise, and she moistened them abstractly. Surely he didn't expect her to meekly follow him? It was equally impossible to imagine she'd been let off the figurative hook.

For a long time she simply stood gazing sightlessly into the exquisitely furnished lounge, and it was only when her eyelids became heavy that she stirred herself sufficiently to douse the lights and make her way towards the other end of the apartment.

Of their own volition her footsteps faltered outside the spare bedroom, and she stood hesitantly unsure for the space of a few seconds before moving inside. Shedding her wrap, she pulled back the coverlet and breathed a faint sigh of relief that the bed was made up, then without further thought she slid in between the pale pink sheets.

When Sachi woke it was light, and long past dawn, if the strength of sunlight streaming in through the slightly parted curtains was any indication.

For a moment she lay still, aware of a wonderful feeling of protective warmth and unable to assimilate its cause.

'Good morning.'

Her eyes flew wide in shocked surprise at the sound of Dominic's soft drawling voice mere inches from her ear, and she twisted her head, her mouth parting in voluble protest at the realisation that she was sharing the large bed in the main bedroom.

'You called out in the middle of the night, and appeared visibly distressed whenever I attempted to leave your side,' he enlightened her quietly, shifting slightly to lie facing her, and his close proximity made her feel frighteningly aware of her own vulnerability. 'It seemed a sensible solution to bring you in here where there was ample room for both of us.'

A haunting drift of partly submerged memory rose to the surface, and she shivered slightly.

'Care to talk about it?'

Oh, God, *no*! They were *her* ghosts—a father consumed by an alcohol-induced rage vilifying everyone on numerous occasions for his loss of fortune; Simone, for her hurtful caustic tongue; and darling Sam, whose pain she couldn't ease.

'I really don't remember.' That much was partly true, for unless she woke in the midst of a particular dream sequence she rarely had any recollection the following morning of what had disturbed her sleep. Besides, she didn't need anyone's sympathy. 'What's the time?' she asked. As a change of subject, it was a banal attempt, and doubtless didn't fool him in the least.

'Just after eight.'

He was so close she could smell the faint muskiness of his skin, actually sense his body warmth. Her pulse rate tripped and the blood began coursing through her veins in recognition of his magnetic sensuality. It was crazy, but she became conscious of every breath she took, every beat of her heart. To remain in bed was madness, yet her limbs seemed temporarily locked into immobility.

'I'll make breakfast.' Her voice sounded so low and husky it was almost inaudible, and the butterflies in her stomach began a series of somersaults as Dominic propped himself on one elbow.

'Why the hurry?'

Because it's too dangerous to stay here, she wanted to scream. 'You mentioned a boat cruise to Sanctuary Cove,' she said on a slightly desperate note, hating the way he affected her equilibrium.

'So I did,' he drawled. 'However, it was only a suggestion.' He lifted a hand and began idly tracing the outline of her jaw, trailing his fingers up to her ear to tuck a stray lock of hair away from her face.

'Dominic—don't! Please,' she added in despair, her eyes wide and luminous as she silently begged him to desist.

'Don't—what?' he taunted softly, bending his head so low over hers she could feel his breath warm against her cheek, and she sensed rather than saw his faint smile an instant before his lips brushed the edge of her mouth. 'Surely you expect to consummate our marriage?'

She looked at him with unblinking clarity, sure that he must feel the heavy beat of her heart as it sent the blood pounding through her veins. 'Yes.'

His mouth curved, parting slightly with deliberate sensuality. 'Yet you're reacting like a frightened little rabbit caught in a trap,' he mused teasingly. As if to prove it, he let his hand slip down to the curve of her breast and felt the rapid acceleration of her pulse. 'What do you imagine is in store for you, Sachi? Pain and degradation?' His lips trailed the path of his hand, light as the brush from a butterfly's wing, before travelling back to settle with infinite provocativeness in the sensitive curve of her neck.

Dear God, she'd never be ready to accept his potent brand of sexuality, yet instinct warned that only a fool would continue to deny him. 'I'm very hungry,' she offered lightly, and watched with bated breath as he lifted his head, barely managing to meet his dark, faintly calculated gaze with seemingly uncontrived solemnity. 'Yesterday food didn't seem to have much priority.'

Was that humour lurking in the depths of his eyes? She fervently hoped so.

'And now it does?'

'Yes.'

'Then by all means let's have breakfast,' Dominic declared smoothly, levering himself to the opposite side of the bed with ease, and Sachi endeavoured to hide her relief as she slid out from between the covers.

A reprieve, even if it was merely temporary, had been granted.

It wasn't until she was dressed, had attended to their unpacking, and had almost finished a wholesome meal of fresh orange juice, muesli and coffee, that she began to wonder if her victory held a hollow tinge.

Dominic was far too astute to be easily fooled, nor could she doubt his ability as a superb strategist in or out of the courtroom. When it came to the *bedroom*, his experience had to be light years ahead of hers. Why had he chosen to retreat, when he could so easily have overcome her resistance?

There was no easy answer, and as she took the elevator down to the ground level she endeavoured to banish an uncanny vision of herself as prey in an animal world with Dominic in the role of a stalking tiger.

CHAPTER SIX

THE Bayview Harbour marina held a variety of moored craft, and it came as no surprise when Dominic helped Sachi aboard a sleek white cruiser whose fitments bore the superb elegance of functional luxury.

'Do you need a hand to cast off?' she called as the engines throbbed into powerful life, and at his nod of assent she followed his instructions to the letter, experiencing a strange thrill of excitement as the cruiser slid from its berth and began heading out towards the channel.

It was years since she had embarked on any pleasurable pursuit. Childhood, an inner voice reminded her. At least she looked the part, attired in neat white cotton shorts and a cotton-knit top, sneakers, and exclusive designer sunglasses shading her eyes from the heat of the midsummer sun.

Dominic looked even more masculine, if that were possible, in navy shorts and a white cotton shirt, his eyes similarly shaded by dark glasses, and he displayed considerable skill in handling the cruiser as it slid effortlessly through the narrow channel towards Paradise Point.

'There's sunscreen cream in one of the galley cupboards,' Dominic advised her as she hovered between exploring the cabin or joining him where he stood at the controls. 'You'll burn very quickly without it.'

Conscious of the truth behind his words, Sachi
quietly slipped down below, found the cream and
applied it, then went back up on deck determined
to enjoy the sun. Her skin was unusually pale,
bearing just the merest hint of a light tan from an
all too brief hour or two at the beach on occasional
weekends.

It took more than a hour to reach Sanctuary
Cove, and as they entered the inner harbour Sachi
was enthralled by the number of pastel-painted,
white-tile-roofed villas hugging the waterfront.
Homes on the hill were veritable mansions, and the
deep cream-painted terrace houses with their pale
sage-green roofs blended beautifully with the tree-
studded background of the Resort's hotel.

Gaining berth at the marina was achieved with
relative ease, and she didn't attempt to hide the
sparkle of anticipation when Dominic suggested
they explore the village shops before settling on any
one of several restaurants for lunch.

In retrospect, it was an idyllic day—one Sachi
felt reluctant to have end, for there were so many
people browsing along the brick-lined lanes that it
wasn't difficult to appear relaxed, even to believe
she could live comfortably within the confines of
a marriage to the man who strolled in companion-
able silence at her side.

Yet almost as soon as they boarded the cruiser
late that afternoon she felt the tension within tighten
her nerves to breaking point—a situation which
seemed to intensify with the traversing of every
nautical mile.

It was past six o'clock when they entered the
Bayview Harbour marina, and Sachi made no

demur when Dominic suggested she go on up to the apartment while he secured the cruiser.

A shower to rid her skin and hair of salt spray was bliss, and after towelling herself dry she donned fresh underwear, then selected a casual skirt and blouse from the wardrobe. Make-up was confined to moisturiser and a touch of colour to her lips, and five minutes with the portable hairdrier restored order to the silky length of her hair.

Dinner? Would they go out, or stay in? Sachi pursed her lips as she pondered the question, wondering whether she should inspect the refrigerator's well-stocked contents and begin preparing a meal.

'We'll eat out.'

Her head snapped up in surprise, for she hadn't even heard Dominic come in.

'Which do you prefer, Sachi? Chinese, Italian, French, Japanese?'

'My goodness, it's all food.' Which it was, and for too many years she had viewed it as essential sustenance rather than with the palate of a gourmet connoisseur.

'You're quite content to leave the booking to mc?'

His faint air of mockery stung, and she met his gaze steadily. 'Somewhere quiet, if you don't mind.'

Dominic lifted a hand to his chin and pulled a rueful face. 'I'll make the call, then shave and shower.'

Sachi had never seen him anything but extremely clean-shaven, but now that she looked there was evidence of darkened shadow along his jaw.

Perhaps she should change? Her attire was hardly suitable for the type of establishment she felt sure Dominic had in mind.

Moving back into the bedroom, she slid open the wardrobe and selected a tailored creation in fashionable black and white, chose elegant high-heeled shoes and matching clutch-purse in white kid, then quickly effected the change. Make-up and re-styling her hair would have to wait until Dominic vacated the adjoining en suite.

At that precise moment he entered the bedroom with a towel knotted carelessly about his hips, the slight musky aroma of his aftershave merely adding to an electrifying awareness of his masculinity.

In desperation Sachi shifted her eyes away from the expanse of muscled chest with its darkened whorls of hair arrowing down to a taut waist. His thighs were long and powerful beneath the towel, and he exuded an animalistic sense of strength from every nerve and fibre.

'If you've finished, I'll retrieve my make-up bag and fix my hair in the other bathroom.' Her voice sounded almost—*prim*, for God's sake!

She caught the faint gleam of amusement in his eyes, and resentment flared deep inside. Damn him! She could almost believe he deliberately sought to provoke.

'Leave your hair loose,' Dominic bade her as he extracted a shirt from the wardrobe and put it on, then beneath her startled gaze he loosened the towel and let it slide to the carpet, selected briefs, then stepped into expensively cut trousers. 'It's more flattering framing your face.'

She opened her mouth to say she'd wear her hair any way she chose, then thought better of it as he took down a belt and threaded it through the narrow keepers at his waist. In an argument he would inevitably emerge the victor, and besides, she was aware of a certain caution in instigating any kind of confrontation.

Without a word she walked through to the en suite where she completed her make-up in record time before wielding a vigorously applied brush to her hair, leaving it loose—*her* decision, she assured herself as she turned back towards the bedroom.

If Dominic glimpsed the faint air of defiance evident in her eyes and the slight tilt of her chin, he gave no indication of it, and in the car they sat in a silence relieved only by muted music flowing from the sophisticated stereo system.

The restaurant he chose was situated only a few kilometres along the broadwater, specialising in a variety of seafood dishes, and each ordered selection proved to be deliciously mouthwatering.

Between courses Sachi searched for a topic of conversation that wouldn't sound incredibly banal. 'It wasn't until yesterday I discovered you have a brother,' she began tentatively. 'Is there anyone other than Brent in your family?'

Dominic lifted his glass and took time to savour the excellent white wine. 'Question and answer time, Sachi?'

She glanced up and caught his dark enigmatic expression, and her eyes widened fractionally as he settled well back in his chair. 'You know every detail about *my* life,' she felt bound to remind him with a trace of defensiveness.

'Both my parents passed away at a relatively early age, and I was left at seventeen with very little except the generosity of an elderly great-aunt who provided Brent and me with a roof over our heads, food in our stomachs, and instilled sufficient self-discipline to ensure that we survived.' He paused, and there was nothing she could gain from his expression. 'As well as being your father's gardener's assistant, I worked a half-shift every night in a bakery, delivered newspapers every morning, and still managed to study. Brent has it easier,' he revealed drily. 'Although at twenty-four, with a few more years of medical school and equal time until he achieves control of his trust fund, he finds life a trifle restricting.'

'And your great-aunt?'

'She died ten years ago.'

'I see,' she said pensively, and glimpsed his slightly cynical smile.

'Do you, Sachi?'

'Yes, I think so.' As a young man, he'd had to fight every inch of the way to achieve success, whereas she had been born into luxury. Yet through fate each had experienced a reversal of circumstances, and in a strange kind of way they were now equal.

The waitress removed their plates and requested an order for dessert, which Sachi declined, opting for coffee and forgoing the cheeseboard.

'Would you like to go on to a nightclub?' Dominic queried several minutes later as he leaned back in his chair and gave every indication of enjoying his coffee. 'Or we could stay here. There's an excellent band and a small dance floor.'

She looked at him carefully, meeting his dark enigmatic gaze with equanimity. 'I can't imagine you feeling comfortable in a nightclub.'

One eyebrow rose in sardonic amusement. 'No?' A faint smile tugged the edge of his mouth. 'Doesn't it fit in with my expected image?'

'That isn't what I meant to imply,' she explained politely. 'I'm sure you lead a very active social existence.'

'Of course,' Dominic drawled. 'My mythical little black book is filled with names of available social-ites just waiting for my invitation to party the night away.'

'One couldn't doubt they exist,' Sachi retorted, directing him a level glance. 'Within the social echelon you just have to be a peer, and until yes-terday, one of the State's—if not the entire country's—most eligible bachelors.'

'My work extends beyond office hours,' he re-minded her with barely concealed mockery. 'And as with most other mortals, I require a minimum six out of the twenty-four hours in which to sleep.'

'Yet you've received media attention at a variety of social functions,' she ventured, and saw his mouth curve with cynical amusement.

'Ah, yes—the ever vigilant Press. They're com-pelled to make copy as part of their profession.' He drained the remainder of his coffee, then cast her an enquiring glance. 'What's it to be, Sachi? There are a number of nightspots we can visit.'

The thought of exchanging this quiet, intimate atmosphere for one filled with society patrons didn't appeal. Although she wasn't quite ready to return to the apartment either, and she fought against in-decision, carefully schooling her features into a mask of thoughtful contemplation. 'Could we walk along the waterfront? There might be a sea breeze.'

'A leisurely evening stroll? After years of duty and social suppression, I thought you'd be eager to make up for lost time.'

Sachi looked at him carefully, searching for the mockery she felt sure must be evident. 'Caring for Sam was never a duty,' she said quietly, aware of the faint prick of tears and equally determined to fight them. It lent her beautiful golden-green eyes a fiery sparkle, and gave her chin a fractional upward tilt that didn't fool the dark partially hooded gaze of the man seated opposite.

Without a word Dominic summoned the waiter for the bill, signed the proffered credit card slip, then stood to his feet.

Sachi followed suit, and outside she walked at his side towards a path that followed the road above the rocky bank guarding the water's edge.

It was a beautiful evening, the sky dark indigo-blue with a sprinkling of stars, and as they rounded the corner the outline of central Surfers' Paradise stood in glorious electricity-lit splendour, its gently curved coastline seeming to project the centre into the sea itself. It was a fascinating sight, and the lights seemed to beckon, pulsing with life and promising excitement.

How far they walked she had no idea, for she was conscious only of the silky-soft lap of water against the rocks, the occasional passing car, and the silent but strangely reassuring presence of the man at her side.

At some stage they must have turned back and retraced their steps, for she became aware of noise from a nearby hotel and had to conceal her surprise when they reached the parked Mercedes.

It was eleven o'clock when Dominic brought the large car to a halt in the Les Colonnades under-ground car park. Sachi registered the time clearly from the dashboard illumination before he switched off the ignition, and it took only a further five minutes to reach the twelfth-floor apartment.

Time enough for the nerves in her stomach to reawaken into frenzied life. Would he sweep her straight into the bedroom, or attempt to reduce her resistance with alcohol in the lounge? Whatever the method, the result was a foregone conclusion, she decided wryly as she preceded him inside, and her heart gave a shaky lurch the instant she heard the door snap closed.

Unable to resist turning her head to look at him, she felt her eyes widen into huge glistening pools as he lifted a hand to her chin, tilting it slightly before lowering his mouth down over hers, drawing gently on the soft warmth within before she could even think to struggle.

Then she was free, and she stood in frozen silence as he brushed his fingers down her cheek before trailing them gently across her parted lips.

'Are you going to provide any resistance?'

Sachi swallowed painfully. 'I'm not sure I can offer any reassurance to the contrary.'

There was a blatant sensuality apparent in his eyes, arousing within her an awareness of intended intimacy that sent shock-waves of frightening magnitude washing through her entire body.

'Out of fear of me?' he pursued softly. 'Or yourself?'

She closed her eyes for all of three seconds, then slowly let her lids flicker open, her eyes brilliantly intense as she met his gaze. 'Go to hell, Dominic!'

'Aren't you just a little afraid I might take you there?'

'I lost any belief in *heaven* playing a part in my salvation long ago!'

Without a further word she turned and walked down the hallway to the main suite, her eyes almost blinded by stupid angry tears. With stiff movements she slipped off her shoes, then she undid the zip fastener on her dress and stepped out of it before reaching for the clip on her bra. Except her fingers fumbled, and she swore beneath her breath.

'Well-brought-up young ladies don't swear,' a voice drawled from behind, and she felt strong fingers free the troublesome clasp with damning ease.

'*This* young lady *does*,' Sachi declared with asperity, not bothering to so much as look at him as she moved through to the adjoining en suite, where, within a few scant minutes, she discarded her slip and briefs, then donned the slinky scrap of satin that passed as a nightgown. Next she retrieved a jar of cleanser from her cosmetic bag and removed every trace of make-up before energetically cleaning her teeth.

Just as she was about to pick up her hairbrush it was taken from her hand, and her gaze locked with Dominic's mirrored reflection as he calmly began to stroke the offending brush through the length of her hair.

He stood head and shoulders above her, his broad muscled frame clearly outlining her slim form, and her eyes openly warred with the lambent warmth reflected in his own.

'Give me the brush.' Her voice was tight with anger and made not the slightest impression, for he merely continued with the self-imposed task, leaving her little choice but to stand in fuming silence until he finished.

'Is there anything else?' Her voice seemed to choke on the words. 'I'd like to go to bed.'

His hands settled over her shoulders and turned her round to face him, lifting her chin to perceive the force of her defiant gaze.

Without a word he caught her close, and she stiffened, defensively resisting such intimate contact. Then her lips parted in a protesting gasp an instant before his mouth took possession of her own.

Expecting an annihilation, she had no defence against the explorative probe of his tongue as it familiarised itself with the inner contours of her mouth, the tender tissues and the highly sensitised surface of her tongue before tasting her lips.

An electrifying awareness tingled through her veins, heightening her senses to an alarming degree as she fought to remain calm beneath an onslaught that became so erotic she began to melt, her body reacting entirely of its own accord as it pressed against his in an instinctive need for closer contact.

Unbidden, her hands crept up his arms to linger at his shoulders before encircling his neck, and she clung to him without thought as he locked her against him.

It seemed an age before his lips left hers and she lifted her head in an attempt to defuse the sheer explosion of warmth that held her in total thrall as his mouth began a slow path down the slender column of her throat to settle in the hollow at the edge of her neck.

Seconds later she gave a soundless gasp as his lips slid down to the creamy softness of her breast, and she was powerless to prevent a cry of protest as he eased her nightgown down over her shoulders and let it slither in a silky heap to the carpeted floor.

'Dominic——' Her plea came to a faltering halt as he sought one roseate peak and savoured it, tantalising with leisurely expertise before trailing slowly to render a similarly evocative treatment to its twin.

She felt as if she was on fire, every nerve-end alive with vibrant life, and she was powerless to utter a sound as he swept her into his arms and walked through to the bedroom.

Sachi became aware of the cool crispness of percale sheets beneath her back, and she closed her eyes against the electric light, silently begging for the protective cover of darkness as his weight depressed the bed.

Slowly, with infinite care, he began an evocative exploration of her body, skilfully knowledgeable of every sensual pleasure-spot, playing each to its fullest sensual pitch until every pore, every nerve-end became suffused with aching warmth.

To lie still in mute acceptance became increasingly impossible, and when his mouth trailed a similar wreaking path she was almost mindless as pleasure radiated throughout her entire body until it became an unbearable all-consuming pain.

Slow silent tears slipped down each cheek as his lips travelled up to her breast, nurturing each hardened peak in turn before possessing her mouth in a deep, passionate kiss that merely served to prolong her own private torture.

Just as she thought she could stand it no longer, he slid his hands beneath her hips, and with consummate skill he coaxed her untutored flesh to accept the full, slow thrust of his masculinity, gentling her wildly threshing limbs as he absorbed her pain before beginning a careful pacing that ultimately took her to the brink of ecstasy, then tipped her over the edge towards a total satiation of the senses.

Afterwards she lay perfectly still, unable to move so much as an inch as he lay down beside her, and she offered no resistance when he gathered her into his arms. She wanted to cry, but no tears would come, and she closed her eyes against his dark discerning gaze.

She should hate him, berate him for effecting such a total violation—not only of her body, but her mind. Except she couldn't find the words.

Later—although how much later, she had little recollection—she felt Dominic slide out of bed, followed seconds later by the sound of running water. It held little impact until he reappeared beside the bed and scooped her into his arms, proceeding despite her protest to carry her down the hallway to the bathroom.

As soon as she glimpsed the partly-filled spa-bath his intention became evident, and she began to struggle in earnest as he stepped into the warm, scented water. It did absolutely no good at all, for his strength far outmatched her own, and within seconds she found herself seated in front of him in the gently pulsing depths, her lower body trapped within the cradle of his thighs.

Holding her wrists with galling ease, he calmly took up soap and began a slow, disruptively sensual cleansing process that encompassed every inch of her skin.

'Must you?' she demanded in a tortured whisper, hating herself for betraying her tenuous emotions.

'Relax,' Dominic drawled as he lifted the hair away from her nape and sponged the pale sensitive skin.

Relax? How could she *relax*, for God's sake, when all her fine body hairs stood on end in damning awareness of him!

'Perhaps you could return the favour.'

Even as she registered his request, he put the sponge in her hand and deftly lifted her round to face him.

'You're expecting too much!' She raised angry eyes to meet his, and felt her body begin to tremble at the slumbrous warmth evident in his expression.

'Am I?' he queried quietly.

'I don't think I'm ready for this,' Sachi choked, despising her own vulnerability as much as the indolent sensual man who provided its cause.

Without a word Dominic put the soap in her hand, covered it with his own, and unhurriedly completed the task. Then he stood to his feet, switched off the jets, and lifted her out to stand on the floor. Before she could voice any protest he reached for a towel and deftly wrapped it round her, then collected another for himself.

'Was that so terrible?'

She clutched the towel as if it was a lifeline to security, for her body felt as if it had been buffeted by an emotional maelstrom of such magnitude she doubted her ability to survive intact. Nothing she had read—not even the most explicit details revealed in journalistic periodicals, nor her wildest imaginings—had prepared her for such a degree of eroticism.

Worse was the knowledge that she could be so easily aroused by a man she professed to dislike.

'Sachi.'

She couldn't bring herself to look at him, and in a moment of desperation she turned away and began to towel the moisture from her body.

Except that she had hardly begun when hands closed over her shoulders and he swung her back to face him. Defiantly she raised stormy eyes bright with the glitter of unshed tears, hating him at that moment for forcing a confrontation.

'What do you want, Dominic?' she demanded, sorely tried. 'A post-mortem of your sexual prowess?'

There was nothing she could discern from his expression, and after a few timeless seconds she was unable to hold his gaze, and her eyelids flickered, then lowered slightly in a gesture of self-defeat.

'I could easily have subjected you to a very different initiation,' he drawled, cupping her chin and tilting it so she had little option but to look at him. 'By taking my own pleasure, slaking my own need, and showing no consideration whatsoever for yours.' His mouth curved into a mocking smile. 'Among the outrage, leave room for a modicum of gratitude.'

Her lips parted to begin a rejoinder, except that the words died in her throat as his mouth closed over hers in a brief, hard kiss, then she was free.

With as much dignity as possible she moved through to the bedroom, exchanged the towel for her nightgown, then slid in between the sheets, aware within seconds of Dominic's presence, and she tensed, unconsciously holding her breath as he settled comfortably within touching distance.

'Goodnight.'

It was impossible to detect anything in his voice, and Sachi didn't even try. Never had she felt so emotionally and physically drained, yet in total variance, *complete*. A satiation of the senses that had everything to do with—*lust*, an inner voice taunted, as she slipped towards the edge of sleep.

When she woke it was daylight, and the tantalising aroma of bacon intermingled with toast and coffee teased her nostrils and made her aware of a ravenous hunger.

A quick glance at her watch on the bedside pedestal revealed that it was almost eight, and she stretched, a luxurious cat-like movement that brought an immediate awareness of slight tension in a number of ill-used muscles, together with a resurgence of memory that made her blush with shame.

To remain in bed was madness, and she quickly pushed aside the sheet, caught up fresh underwear, shorts and a bright pink top and effected a rapid change before crossing to the en suite, where she sluiced her face with cold water and cleaned her teeth. A vigorous application of the brush restored her hair to a gleaming mantle of silk, and she simply twisted its length into a careless knot on top of her head.

The thought of having to face Dominic made her feel weak at the knees, and only sheer determination lent her limbs the impetus to walk calmly through to the kitchen.

He glanced up from the task of transferring the contents of a frying pan on to plates, and directed her a slow indolent smile.

'Good morning.' How was it possible to sound so—*normal*, when inside she was consumed by a multitude of emotions too difficult to define? 'Hungry?'

'Yes,' Sachi acknowledged evenly to a point just above his right shoulder. As crazy as it seemed, she was unable to look directly at him, and it irked her considerably that he knew precisely why.

He laughed—a soft husky sound that emerged from the depths of his throat. 'Be a good girl and pour the coffee, will you?'

Sachi felt inclined to tell him to do it himself, except that such an action was childish, and she had no particular desire to appear anything remotely juvenile. 'How do you have it?' she asked politely as she crossed to the percolator and began dispensing the rich aromatic brew into two mugs.

'Black, no sugar.'

Sachi ate the two eggs and four rashers of bacon on her plate, together with two slices of toast and a small glass of freshly squeezed orange juice.

'That's the first time I've seen you enjoy a meal in my presence,' Dominic drawled as she refilled both mugs with coffee and carried them to the table.

'I could plead an extreme case of bridal jitters as the cause,' she offered, and glimpsed slight amusement evident in his smile.

'Which no longer exist?'

How could she answer no, when her whole body felt like a finely tuned instrument? Even thinking about the sensations his touch had evoked set her nerve-ends tingling, stimulating every sensory pulsebeat until, unbidden, her breathing quickened and a shiver feathered its way down the length of her spine.

'Would you settle for a non-committal response?'

Dominic laughed softly, and one glance at those gleaming dark eyes revealed that he wasn't fooled in the slightest. 'Choose how you'd like to spend the day, Sachi,' he drawled. 'My appearance in court tomorrow necessitates a return to Brisbane tonight.'

'Sea World,' she said at once, opting for one of the Coast's most popular theme parks. It was years since she'd indulged in anything remotely frivolous, and besides, it gave her a wicked sense of pleasure in choosing something so obviously tourist-orientated. 'If you don't mind, of course.'

One eyebrow rose in mocking amusement. 'I wouldn't dream of objecting.'

'Really?' It was impossible to curb a widening smile as she stood up from the table. 'And the dishes?'

'All yours,' he said with sardonic emphasis. 'I cooked breakfast.'

CHAPTER SEVEN

IN RETROSPECT, it was a carefree day and one Sachi was reluctant to see come to a close. The dolphins and sea-lions were a delight to watch, and for the space of a few hours she felt like a child again as she lapsed into spontaneous laughter over the trained antics of the various sea-creatures.

It wasn't until they had showered, packed, dined at a superb restaurant in an exclusive hotel resort on the Spit, and were speeding through the night towards Brisbane, that Sachi became consumed with restless apprehension.

Soon they would be home, and once there her life as Dominic's wife would begin in earnest. The thought of being launched into leading an active social existence was daunting, and she wasn't sufficiently foolish as to imagine there would be a lack of gossip regarding her new status. The past—more pertinently her father's path from riches to rags—would be dragged out into the open and doubtless embellished.

A faint sigh whispered from her lips as she let her head sink back against the cushioned headrest.

'One hardly dares ask,' Dominic's voice invaded the car's dim interior, and she spared him a startled glance in realisation that he had heard that faint sound.

'Reality,' Sachi responded simply, unsure whether he would assume the role of ally or enemy. As his wife, surely she could rely on some measure of loyalty?

'You're well equipped to deal with it.'

After last night, she would never be equipped to deal with *him*. And what of tonight? Would he expect a willing pupil in his bed, eager to taste every sensual delight?

She looked at his strong profile as it became outlined by passing headbeams of light, and suppressed a faint shiver. There was an animalistic sense of power apparent, an inherent vitality that created an aura of supreme indomitability and merely enhanced a claim to more than his share of dynamic masculinity.

Dear lord in heaven! she groaned inwardly. She'd have to pull herself together, otherwise Dominic might guess the state of her emotions, and that would be unbearable.

Perhaps if she closed her eyes he would think she'd lapsed into a light doze, and that way she would be spared having to make conversation. Certainly the soft music emitting from the stereo speakers promoted relaxation, and soon there was no need for pretence.

'Sachi, we're home.'

She woke at once, instantly focusing on the strength of his features outlined in stark relief by the bright internal lights of the large garage. Without a word she reached for the doorclasp and slid out from the passenger seat.

The house seemed to extend an unspoken welcome as she followed Dominic indoors, and she watched in silence as he deposited their bags at the foot of the stairs.

'I'll need to check the messages on my answering machine,' he told her with a certain wryness.

'Shall I make coffee and bring yours into the study?'

'Please.' He shot her a perceptive glance that was far too discerning for her peace of mind. 'I could be tied up for an hour or two.'

'I'll unpack,' Sachi declared decisively. 'Besides, it's quite late, and I'm tired.' With luck she'd already be asleep by the time he joined her in bed. After last night she doubted she could cope with another lesson in lovemaking.

Lust, she amended cynically as she entered the kitchen and set about making the coffee. To imagine what they had shared as being anything other than a physical slaking of the senses was beyond comprehension. Part of her felt sickened by the degree of pleasure she had experienced, while buried deep within her sensuous soul lay another which luxuriated in sheer voluptuous sensation.

She should hate him—and she did, she assured herself fervently upon leaving the study, his drawled 'goodnight' barely concealing a degree of amusement that positively rankled.

The feeling of antipathy remained as she unpacked, then showered, and even in bed she lay seething, unable to relax sufficiently to enable an easy escape into somnolence.

It seemed an age before Sachi heard the quiet, almost inaudible sound of Dominic's entry into the bedroom, and she lay perfectly still, deliberately pacing her breathing so it would appear she slept— no mean acting feat when it felt as if her heart would leap through her chest the instant he slid into bed.

For a few breathless minutes she thought she had been sufficiently convincing, and just as she began to relax he reached out and gathered her slim form into the curve of his body.

'I was asleep,' she muttered in protest, pushing ineffectually at the hands clasping her waist.

'Liar,' he drawled close to her temple, and a curious weakness invaded her limbs, bringing with it a heightened sexual tension that tripped her pulse and sent the blood pounding through her veins.

She could smell the faint muskiness of his after-shave as his lips trailed across her cheek in a downward path towards her mouth. If he kissed her, she'd be lost, and she wasn't sure she was capable of resisting his disruptive brand of sensuality.

Maybe if he thought she was uninterested... A tiny derisive laugh rose and died in her throat. Who was she attempting to fool? Besides, her body was its own traitorous mistress, and she didn't doubt he would take pleasure in overcoming any physical resistance she might provide.

'Do you intend taking advantage of your conjugal rights *every* night?' she snapped.

She tensed as his fingers slid the straps of her nightgown off one shoulder, and seconds later the breath caught painfully in her throat as his mouth teased a path to her breast, where, much to her chagrin, she was powerless to prevent the burgeoning of its peak in anticipation of his possession.

A fierce ache began in the pit of her stomach and rapidly spiralled until it affected every single nerve-ending, making it increasingly difficult to fight against his sensual onslaught.

'Dominic——' His name left her lips as a hollow groan that combined protest and a certain amount of anguished resignation.

'You want me to stop?'

The words whispered softly against her cheek as his lips trailed upwards to outline its delicate bonestructure, and she turned her head involuntarily as she sought that taunting, provocative mouth with her own, issuing a silent invitation as old as Eve herself in the delicate arch of her body, the sensuous exploration of her hands as they traced his ribcage, the lean line to his hips and the flat musculature of his stomach.

His mouth firmed and became flagrantly seductive as it coaxed hers, seeking a generous unbidden response that seemed totally beyond her control. Not content, he deliberately aroused each pleasure spot until her entire body was consumed with liquid fire, and she became mindless, floating in a world of sensuality so intense there was no room for anything except the swirling vortex into which she had been drawn.

Even then there was no relief, nor the release she craved as his mouth left hers to begin a destructively slow downward path, and she gasped at the brazen degree of intimacy he seemed intent on taking, her shocked cry of outraged disbelief very real as he took what she considered to be an impossible liberty.

Her hands sought his head, her fingers curling into the dark hair to tug with maddening frenzy as tumultuous sensation washed over her, each successive wave more intense than the last until there were no bounds, and on the point of total satiation she sensed rather than felt his shift in weight, then his mouth covered hers as the rhythmic pattern of his movements created a deep, throbbing ache so acute that she cried out against such a degree of sensual pleasure.

It was a long time before she lay still, so overcome with listless inertia that the slightest movement was an intolerable effort. Her eyelids fluttered closed, their silky lashes suspiciously damp from tears she had little recollection of shedding, and she wanted to turn on her side and curl her body into a foetal curve, protected as she slept and sheltered from any further sexual invasion.

If last night had been instrumental in her sexual awakening, tonight was a total devastation of the senses.

Perhaps the most painful revelation of all was the knowledge that she had become a craving wanton in Dominic's arms, begging his possession in a manner that made her burn with mortifying shame.

On the edge of sleep she was aware of the cradling strength of his arms, the soft brush of his lips against her forehead, then she was claimed by sheer exhaustion.

When Sachi woke it was daylight, and she was alone with only the rumpled sheets and the imprint of a male head on the pillow beside her own to remind her that Dominic had shared her bed.

It was, she determined with a lazy glance at the bedside clock, well after nine—a time that almost sent her scurrying to her feet in mindless panic. Except that memory surfaced, and with it came the knowledge that although Dominic was assuredly ensconced behind his desk in the city, *she* could look forward to a day of leisure. If one discounted the necessity to ensure that all her belongings were intact and unpacked, a need to establish some kind of rapport with Janet Armitage over household matters and the preparation of their evening meal—not to mention supervision of alterations carried out on the master bedroom suite by one of Poissant's most revered tradesmen. Which, from the sound of it, had already begun, she decided, as measured hammering reverberated through the adjoining walls.

On reflection, it was a most satisfying day, and as she put the finishing touches to the table Sachi mused that she couldn't be more pleased with the way the alterations were shaping up. Janet Armitage had proved herself to be a charming woman, friendly in a motherly kind of way with what appeared to be a genuine interest in following her mistress's wishes, and after she had thoroughly explored every room in the house and made an extensive scrutiny of the grounds, there was a tremendous sense of contentment and familiarity in being *home* again. The only problem she had was coming to terms with her position as Dominic's wife.

Her hand trembled visibly as she put the last piece of cutlery down on the table. Within a few minutes the Mercedes would whisper to a halt at the edge of the driveway—then *what*? Would Dominic want a drink first, followed by a shower, before dinner? Or the reverse? Perhaps he'd opt for a swim in the pool, followed by a shower, then a drink. Oh, dear God, *why* was she such a mass of nerves?

Because, a tiny voice taunted, you refuse to recognise that the childish adoration you cherished all those years ago has never really died, and you're afraid—yes, *afraid*, to even begin to analyse if there might be a deeper motive behind Dominic's insistence that marriage to him was your only solution.

Damn it, she cursed shakily, introspection of any kind was positively dangerous. Already it was drawing her into an emotional vortex from which she had to fight to escape if she wanted to retain a degree of sanity.

With determined resolve she switched on the television and steadfastly fixed her attention on the broadcast news.

Half an hour later she resembled a quivering wreck, and when the telephone rang she jumped with fright before flying into the hallway to answer its insistent summons.

'Sachi? I should be home in twenty minutes.'

She must have said something, but he had replaced the receiver before the words left her lips. Damn, the carefully planned menu she'd consulted with Janet and helped prepare would begin to lose its flavour if she didn't take action. Dessert, comprising fresh fruit, wouldn't matter at all, but the tangy apricot sauce accompanying the delicately sautéd chicken would have to be reheated. The assortment of vegetables could be stir-fried as she boiled the rice.

With deft movements she removed dishes, heated the oven, checked the herb bread, and dithered over the choice of wine. Never had she felt so damned nervous—not even on her first night as waitress at the Patrullo family restaurant.

Then she heard the faint clunk of the car door closing, quickly followed by footsteps crossing the veranda, and she lifted a hand to her hair, unconsciously smoothing its length as she moved through the lounge to greet him.

'Dominic.' Her eyes flew straight to his strongly-defined features, noting the faint lines creasing his brow, the deeply etched grooves slashing each cheek. 'How was your day?' The words left her lips as a politely voiced query, and she glimpsed his wry smile as he deposited his briefcase on to a nearby side-table.

'Genuine interest, Sachi?' he slanted with barely concealed mockery. 'Or merely a polite conversational gambit?'

'Oh, conversation,' she said at once, forcing a bright smile, and she bore his hard piercing gaze with equanimity, although her eyes changed from hazel to molten gold. 'Shall I get you a drink?'

'Please,' he drawled. 'A small measure of whisky, with a generous splash of soda.'

Sachi crossed to the cabinet and extracted a glass, added ice, then seconds later she retraced her steps and solemnly handed him the half-filled crystal tumbler.

'Won't you join me? A light wine, perhaps?'

'I'd prefer to wait until dinner.'

He lifted a hand and loosened his tie, then drained the contents of his tumbler in one long swallow before setting it down on a nearby table. 'I'll take a shower, then change. Shall we say dinner in ten minutes?'

Sachi nodded, then stood in shocked surprise as he dropped a brief hard kiss on her unsuspecting mouth before moving with an easy litheness from the room.

The meal was superb, and part of her felt a certain pleasure in witnessing his enjoyment of the food.

'I've arranged for a car to be delivered tomorrow,' Dominic informed her as he selected segments of fresh fruit and transferred them into his mouth. 'For your use.'

She pushed her plate to one side. 'Why? My own should be ready soon.'

'I don't consider that particular vehicle to be sufficiently reliable. When the mechanics have finished with it, it can be sold.'

'Doesn't a rather rusty disreputable aged sedan fit in with the required image?'

Dominic settled back in his chair, removed his napkin and put it on the table. 'Precisely what *image* are we discussing?' His voice was as smooth as silk and infinitely dangerous.

'Yours,' said Sachi without thought. 'Or rather, mine, as your wife.'

'Ah, you see yourself as one of my possessions, is that it?' he queried softly. 'Given the requisite jewellery, clothes, *car*, in which to be suitably displayed.'

'Isn't that your intention?'

'Why not simply accept?' he parried, watching her through faintly narrowed eyes. 'Most women would delight——'

'I won't be *bought*, damn you!' Sachi was so furious it was all she could do not to pick up something and throw it at him. Yet even as she considered it, the truth of her own hastily flung words settled with bitter irony. He *had* bought her—almost literally.

Sickened, she rose to her feet. 'I'm going for a walk.'

'Where, precisely? It's almost dark.'

She looked at him, her eyes locking with his in silent warring battle. 'I don't *care* where! It's enough that I get away from you and everything you stand for!'

'In that case, take Sheikh with you. He'll enjoy the exercise.'

'*You* exercise him. I'm going alone.'

'No,' Dominic reiterated softly, and without thought Sachi picked up a crystal flute and threw it at him, seeing his reflex action in seemingly terrifying slow motion as he deflected it, followed by a soft thud as the flute fell to the carpeted floor behind him. 'Pity,' he drawled. 'It was one of a pair.'

Without a word she stood to her feet and walked through to the kitchen where she began systematically stacking dishes. Her fingers shook with nervous tension, and twice a plate almost slipped to the floor as she began loading the dishwasher. Damn! *Damn* him! she cursed beneath her breath. He really was the most remorseless man she'd ever met, and his very calm made her want to scream in silent rage against him.

A slight movement on the edge of her peripheral vision made her glance towards the opposite end of the kitchen, and her attention was arrested by Dominic in the process of placing an assortment of plates, cutlery and serving dishes on to the servery bench.

'Will you give me your word that you won't venture out of the grounds?' Sachi didn't trust herself to speak, and he continued hardily, 'If not, be warned I'll activate the security system and command Sheikh to restrain any attempt you make to leave.'

'That's tantamount to imprisonment!' she said furiously, scandalised that he would contemplate such an action.

'You're free to go wherever you choose as long as you observe sensible precautions.'

'Conditions,' she amended, and glimpsed the cynical humour beneath the hard lines strengthening his features.

'If it's merely anger you need to get out of your system, I'll oppose you in a set of tennis.' A wry smile curved his mouth. 'You can vent your excessive energy by slamming the ball in my direction.' One eyebrow rose in sardonic query. 'Shall we say an hour from now?'

'By then I'll have simmered down,' Sachi responded trenchantly, her eyes wary as he closed the distance between them. 'Besides, you'd easily win against me.'

Dominic reached out and caught hold of her chin between thumb and forefinger. 'Is it so important that you win?'

Sachi swallowed painfully, her eyes still stormy. 'It's important that I don't lose.'

Dark eyes gentled and assumed a mocking gleam. 'The tennis court, in an hour. Brent will be down at the weekend.' He smiled, revealing strong white teeth. 'Regard it as necessary practice for any upcoming social soirée.' He turned and walked from the kitchen, and she stood staring at his departing back until he had moved out of sight.

With the dishes attended to, the kitchen and dining-room restored to pristine order, there was no other course but to go upstairs and sort through her wardrobe for something suitable in which to play tennis.

It was obvious that Nicole had been extremely thorough in carrying out Dominic's instructions, Sachi determined, for there was an assortment of designer tennis gear from which to choose, right down to socks and footwear.

Anger rose to the surface, and her lips tightened as she selected a skirt and top at random before pulling on a pair of socks. It rankled unbearably that every conceivable aspect of her wearing apparel had been catered for, except, it appeared, sporting accessories, and specifically a racquet. Something Dominic would have to provide, she decided as she made her way downstairs minutes before the appointed time.

The court was floodlit, its synthetic surface professionally smooth, and Sachi felt her stomach complete a series of erratic somersaults as she crossed to where Dominic stood, racquets in hand, looking every inch the leisure-bent male sophisticate attired in casual shorts and an open-necked shirt.

'It's ages since I last played,' she cautioned, half fearful she would make a complete fool of herself.

'All it takes is practice,' Dominic dismissed, handing over a racquet. 'Try that.'

He could, Sachi determined almost an hour later, easily have beaten her, even if she was in top form. Yet his play was controlled as he returned the ball across the net with measured strokes when it was only too apparent that he possessed the skill and ability to power any opponent off the court.

'A swim?' he suggested.

The thought of cooling off in the sparkling, blue-tiled pool was infinitely tempting, and Sachi walked at his side to where changing-rooms were positioned between the tennis court and the pool.

'Janet ensures that there's a supply of towels on hand,' Dominic drawled as she cast him a quick enquiring glance, and his eyes assumed a faintly wicked gleam. 'The pool is quite private. Whatever you're wearing beneath that skirt and top will provide adequate covering.'

A faint blush crept over her cheeks. 'I was considering nudity, actually.' If she'd hoped to shock him, she failed dismally, for all it earned was a slightly raised eyebrow.

'Provocation, Sachi? Are you confident of being able to handle the consequences?'

'You,' she seethed, her eyes a blaze of gold, 'are impossible!'

'So I've been told,' he returned blandly.

'By countless female acquaintances,' she returned without contrition, and heard his husky laughter.

'I haven't had the time or the inclination to be a rake,' he slanted, shooting her a quizzical glance.

'You're no monk.' The words slipped out without thought, and his mouth curved to form a faintly wry, mocking smile.

'You want me to reveal details of every woman I've bedded since puberty, Sachi?'

'*I* have no past, no former——' She faltered to a halt, incredibly angry that there had been no man in her life before him, no one with whom to compare the utter devastation he was able to wreak with her fragile emotions.

'Lovers?' he finished silkily, and his eyes narrowed faintly at the tide of colour that washed over her cheeks. 'Does it bother you that I've enjoyed the company of other women?'

Oh, God, he didn't pull any punches! Why did she suddenly feel so close to tears? With a contrived, careless shrug, she forced a slight smile, although her eyes assumed the brilliant hue of topaz. 'A simple yes or no, Dominic? Either one would incriminate me, and I refuse to give you that satisfaction.' Dropping down to one knee, she unlaced and removed her sneakers, then her socks. Next came her skirt, quickly followed by its matching top.

A few swift steps and she dived into the pool, surfacing halfway down its length. She swam like a fish, long graceful strokes that employed an economy of movement, yet with sufficient strength to give her enviable speed.

All she could think of was a need to expend an excess of nervous energy, and, uncaring of the man who stripped down to hipster briefs before joining her in the pool, she covered several lengths until choosing to rest at the tiled edge, aware of his powerful frame as he swam effortlessly to her side.

'Had enough?'

The water lapped her shoulders, a cool translucent blue reflected by underwater illumination. She was conscious of the transparency of her attire, the paleness of her skin in contrast to his, and frighteningly aware of the utter frailty of her female form.

'I've accepted a dinner invitation tomorrow evening,' Dominic declared with drawling cynicism. 'One of those glittering occasions benefiting a worthwhile charity with a guest list reading like a veritable *Who's Who* of the city's social echelons.'

Sachi's heart sank, and the nerves in her stomach began to flutter with anxiety. 'You want me to shine, I imagine, attired in something horrendously expensive with an exclusive designer label that will be immediately evident to every woman in the room.' She turned her head slightly and aimed a wry smile in the vicinity of his right cheekbone. 'Perhaps you'd better examine my wardrobe for something suitable. If nothing meets with your approval, I'll have to embark on another shopping expedition.' Her smile intensified, assuming a definite tinge of mockery. 'Not to mention a session with a beauty salon to take care of my hair, make-up and nails. I'll definitely need the entire day.'

His answering smile was equally mocking. 'Do whatever you please—with one exception. Leave your hair loose.'

'I thought something sleekly upswept in a style that will accentuate my appearance as a delicate porcelain doll.'

'Don't be facetious,' he chided sardonically.

'What if I elect to rebel?' Sachi countered without guile, and glimpsed a faint hardening in those dark eyes inches above her own.

'I wouldn't advise it.'

She felt an involuntary shiver that had nothing to do with the water temperature. 'What should I expect, Dominic? A sound spanking for insubordination?'

'Something infinitely more subtle.' He smiled, a mere facsimile that chilled her very bones.

'I think I'll shower and change,' Sachi voiced tightly, levering herself out from the pool. Gathering up a towel, she wound it around her sarong-fashion, then quickly made her way back to the house.

He was a total enigma, she determined. Apparently sensitive and caring one moment, then compellingly ruthless the next. It was almost as if he was playing a manipulative game, with himself as puppeteer.

It wasn't a feeling she enjoyed, and anger surged to the surface at the thought of appearing on his arm tomorrow evening, the personification of elegance, expected to charm everyone in sight with her wit and intelligence.

For a moment she considered dressing in something incredibly outlandish and behaving in the most awful gushing manner. Except that an ingrained sense of self-worth made her cringe at exploiting herself in such a way. And if that wasn't sufficient deterrent, Dominic's expected reaction had a crushing effect. Whether it be a show of strength or verbal war, he would undoubtedly emerge the winner, and she was damned if she'd allow him the slightest victory.

No, she'd play it his way, she determined as she entered the en suite adjacent to their bedroom and turned on the taps in the shower cubicle. And she'd choose something quite different from the gowns Nicole had helped her select. The image she wanted to project was that of a cool sophisticate, assured and completely at ease with the society with which Dominic consorted. She had seen precisely what she wanted on the rack of an exclusive boutique. With luck, it would still be there tomorrow.

Half an hour later, deliciously warm, her hair washed and dry, she slid in between the sheets to lie correlating possible accessories to go with the gown of her choice.

'You look remarkably pensive,' remarked Dominic as he moved towards his side of the bed, and she turned her head slightly, hastily averting her eyes from his naked frame as he shrugged off his towelling robe.

'Like most females, I'm giving considerable thought to what I intend wearing tomorrow evening,' she responded without guile, and caught the laughing gleam apparent in the depths of his eyes as he tossed aside the sheet and slid into bed.

'Right at this moment,' he drawled, reaching for her, 'all I'm concerned about is what you're *not* wearing.'

For her own sake she had to project an icy façade. 'Who would guess that beneath the impeccable Zegna suiting and cool legal brain lies an animalistic male with an insatiable sexual appetite?'

His husky laughter was infuriating. 'Not all my suits are styled by that famed Italian designer. And, my sweet innocent wife, if I were sexually insatiable I would selfishly consider my own satisfaction and care not at all whether I gave pleasure in return.'

Unable to look at him, Sachi turned her head away, only to have her chin captured and forced to meet his gaze.

She was helplessly angry, and she didn't fully understand why. 'What follows next? A lesson in how to pleasure my mentor?' Her eyes glittered with animosity. 'I know I'm not ready for it.'

A faintly twisted smile pulled the edges of his mouth, and his expression was infinitely mocking. 'Inhibitions, Sachi? Aren't you in the least curious to discover the power a woman can have over a man?'

She looked at him carefully, seeing the sheer masculine beauty in the sculptured bone-structure, the strength and depth in those dark gleaming eyes, the sensual curve of his mouth.

'I don't think any woman could completely tame you,' she opined with undue solemnity, knowing it to be the truth. 'You might allow her to think she has, but there would always be a slight element of doubt.' Something that would maintain a touch of mystery in the relationship and keep his partner on her toes, ensuring that he was never taken totally for granted. And if his partner was sufficiently clever, *she* would dare to do the same.

'Afraid I might issue a challenge, Sachi?'

His face was much too close to hers for comfort, and she swallowed painfully. 'It wouldn't do any good,' she said shakily, and sensed rather than heard his soft laughter the instant before his mouth covered hers in a kiss that dissolved any vestige of resistance and sent her clinging to him in willing supplication.

CHAPTER EIGHT

THE charity dinner was an outstanding success, judging by the number of various city luminaries present, Sachi perceived as she glanced idly around the large room.

Women silently vied with each other as to who was the most exclusively gowned and coiffured, and a king's ransom in jewellery could be seen displayed in glittering adornment.

As Dominic Preston's wife, she sensed the circumspect speculation evident and endeavoured to enact an expected part—one that was clearly successful, for her smile was warm and guileless, her interest apparently genuine as introductions were effected and drinks dispensed, along with an interesting selection of canapés and hors d'oeuvre.

'Dazzling,' Dominic accorded with gleaming humour in a quiet aside.

'My gown?' Her eyes positively sparkled as she took an appreciate sip of excellent champagne. 'I'm so pleased you approve. It was ruinously expensive.' She offered him a particularly sweet smile. 'Enough to have kept me in food for a year, in fact.'

Figure-hugging, it was far removed from the classic 'little black dress' most women considered an essential addition to their wardrobe. Definitely a *creation*, it moulded her slim curves to perfection, a width of stiffened silk banding each shoulder adding elegance to what otherwise would have been a strapless bodice, and the hemline was knee-length. Encased in sheer hose, her legs appeared shapely and incredibly slender, while her feet were expensively clad in Jourdan black suede leather evening shoes.

Her jewellery consisted of a diamond pendant on an exquisitely fine gold chain, with matching diamond ear-studs. A belated wedding gift, Dominic had assured her upon presenting them to her only minutes before they were due to leave the house. Her refusal to accept had been firmly overruled, and her politely voiced 'thank you' was negated by the faint stirring of anger at being forced to conform.

Now her eyes slid over his tall frame in silent admiration. His tailoring was impeccable, his dress-shirt starkly white in contrast with his dark evening suit, and there was an innate sophistication apparent that made him stand apart from everyone else in the room.

Which was crazy, Sachi decided. There were any number of men present who were equally prominent in wealth and position, yet few bore Dominic's dramatic mesh of male charisma and self-assurance. Aware of it or not, he managed to project an enviable aura of power which, combined with elemental sensuality, provided a tangible magnet in his attraction to women.

He seemed to have the strangest effect on her senses, making her aware of an elusive alchemy that she found vaguely frightening. There were times when she wished they'd married for all the right reasons, instead of——

'Have I suddenly grown horns?' Dominic drawled, and she lowered her gaze to fasten fixedly on his immaculate bow tie.

'Of course not.' She summoned forth a brilliant smile. 'I was merely attempting to assess what it is about you that brings women to your side like bees buzzing round a honeypot.'

His lips twisted with ill-concealed humour. 'Not my rugged good looks?'

Sachi gave every pretence of subjecting him to an analytical appraisal. 'I suppose you *are* handsome in an aloof, ruthless fashion. And you *do* possess a body any athlete would kill for,' she considered, tilting her head slightly to one side.

Dominic lifted a hand to brush light fingers down the edge of her cheek. 'Stay in the shallows, darling,' he chided gently, and she let her eyes widen with deliberate guile.

'But I swim exceptionally well.'

'Uncharted depths can be dangerous,' he mocked as he let his hand drop down to catch hold of her wrist. Seconds later his thumb began a disturbing pattern across the sensitive veins, creating havoc with her equilibrium.

'Must you?' Sachi demanded in a fierce whisper, hating the way her body responded to his touch.

'We're newlyweds, remember?'

'That doesn't mean you have to—*devour* me!'

'Is that what I'm doing?'

He sounded genuinely amused, damn him! 'Shouldn't we circulate?' Sachi countered. 'I'm sure there are figurative knives aimed at my back, and it would seem infinitely more sensible to be a moving target than a sitting duck.'

His eyes narrowed faintly, and his expression became infinitely sardonic. 'Your imagination appears to be working overtime.'

'Really?' she queried lightly, and, lifting the fluted glass to her lips, she sipped the last of her champagne. 'Perhaps I should attempt to charm your male associates,' she declared fearlessly. 'It might prove entertaining.'

'Don't begin games you have no intention of pursuing,' Dominic cautioned drily. 'Not everyone abides by the rules.'

'And you do?'

He lifted her hand to his lips, caressing the open palm with erotic deliberation as his eyes issued a silent warning. 'You can always count on my honesty.'

For the space of a few seconds she was totally unaware of their fellow guests or the muted background music. She and Dominic could have been alone in time, immune from the outside world.

'Dom, *darling*!'

Sachi registered the sultry feminine tones, and she turned her head slowly, fascinated to see if the voice matched her visual concept.

It did, for the woman was arresting, model slim, tall and blonde with perfect features, a ravishing smile, and brilliant green eyes that clung to Dominic with such tenacious hunger that Sachi began to think he might easily be eaten alive.

'Whatever is this I hear about you being——' the blonde paused imperceptibly '—*married*?' A moue pulled the perfectly painted mouth. 'Tell me it's nothing more than a vicious rumour.'

'Sachi, allow me to introduce you to the wife of one of my associates,' drawled Dominic without blinking so much as an eyelid. 'Michelle Sanderson.'

'Michelle,' Sachi acknowledged politely, and attempted to tug her hand free of his grasp without success.

'Should I know you?' the beautiful blonde persisted. 'We don't seem to have met before.'

'My wife is an interior decorator,' Dominic informed her smoothly. 'Up until now, her work has been her consuming passion.'

'Really?' One perfectly pencilled eyebrow rose to form a graceful arch. 'Which firm are you with?'

It afforded Sachi the utmost pleasure to reveal the name of her employers, and she glimpsed the faint surprise evident in Michelle's expression before it was successfully masked.

'I might offer you a commission.'

There could be no doubt it was meant to be an enormous favour bestowed, and Sachi inclined her head in apparent gratitude.

'I was only telling James the other day that we simply *must* do something with the guest wing. I'll call you, shall I?'

'Please do,' invited Sachi. 'The number is in the book.'

At that precise moment an announcement was made advising guests that dinner was about to be served.

Dominic placed an arm about Sachi's waist and gave Michelle a brief dismissing nod. 'If you'll excuse us?'

The various courses were superbly presented, and after sipping another glass of champagne, Sachi felt capable of dealing with anything—even the rather obvious probing of a society matron bent on extracting sufficient information to use as gossip.

'Tarrant? That should ring a bell. Not *the* Tarrant—Simon Tarrant?' Her double chin almost quivered in expectation of such a juicy titbit. 'You are one of his daughters?' Eyes hardened measurably before assuming a calculating gleam. 'What a strange coincidence that you should recently have married the new owner of your former home!'

'Yes, isn't it?' Sachi agreed sweetly, and if an Oscar for acting ability was being handed out, she most assuredly deserved one for the adoring look she cast Dominic. 'Darling, you must tell Mrs Grenville how you swept me to the altar in just over a week.' To compound the situation, she glanced back towards the lady in question, and declared dreamily, 'He really is such a romantic! You'd imagine a barrister to be—well, *staid*, wouldn't you?' She permitted a soft breathy sigh to escape her lips. 'But he's——' She trailed to a halt, then turning towards Dominic she lavished him with a melting glance. 'Devastating.'

If Sachi hoped to cause him embarrassment, she failed dismally, for without missing a beat he directed her a dazzling smile, then he caught hold of her hand and carried it to his lips, taking time to kiss each finger in turn. 'I wasn't prepared to take the slightest chance of having you escape from me.'

This brought polite laughter, a few overt glances, and, Sachi fervently prayed, little conjecture. Details of her father's tragic death had been splashed across a number of state tabloids, and it was only a matter of time before a few memories were jolted and the gossip train gathered momentum.

'They're playing my favourite kind of music,' Sachi murmured lightly as she placed a beautifully manicured hand on Dominic's forearm. 'Could we dance, do you think?'

The look he directed her was so intimate it was all she could do not to blush, and when they reached the dance floor he enfolded her much too close against him for her peace of mind. So close she couldn't help but be aware of his arousal as they moved slowly together, and she fought down her own awakening desire with a deliberate attempt at anger.

'What are you trying to prove?' she hissed between clenched teeth, and felt his chest reverberate with silent laughter.

'Why, *darling*,' he teased in an unmerciful undertone, 'merely demonstrating that I can't wait to get you home and into our bed.' His lips teased her temple before slipping down to her ear. 'Isn't that the image you're attempting to project? Or am I reading from a different scenario?'

'I don't want to be seen merely as an acquisition that's convenient in your life.'

'Really, Sachi,' Dominic chided softly, 'why should anyone think that?'

'Do you have any conception of how it feels being *displayed* among these people?' Sachi felt as if her nerves were stretched to their tautest limitation. 'I can almost hear what they're thinking!'

His dark glance speared through to her very soul. 'If it distresses you to that extent, we'll leave.'

'Sympathy, Dominic?' she queried with more than a hint of bitterness, and saw his eyes harden.

'Try—compassion.'

'What about other occasions? Will you be so compassionate then?'

'The past can't be changed,' he declared drily. 'And the future can only be dealt with one day at a time.'

'To be so incredibly logical must be a tremendous asset,' she remarked with intended mockery, and glimpsed his cynical smile.

'A necessity for a member of the legal fraternity, wouldn't you say?'

Sachi refrained from comment, and when the music came to an end she preceded Dominic to their table. The thought of maintaining an entirely false façade for what remained of the evening was infinitely wearying, and besides, she had the beginnings of a headache.

'I'd like to leave, if you don't mind,' she pleaded quietly, and felt incredibly relieved when he acceded without demur.

In the car she sat in silence, her eyes fixed beyond the windscreen as Dominic sent the luxurious vehicle purring through the city streets towards suburban Hamilton, and once inside the grounds he activated the remote device controlling the automatic garage door.

Sachi turned towards him in stunned disbelief as he brought the Mercedes to a halt alongside a gleaming white Honda Prelude.

'Yours,' he drawled. 'The keys are in the ignition.'

It was beautiful, and she said so, unable to withhold her pleasure. 'Thank you.'

'Treat it as an early Christmas gift,' Dominic declared as she ran her hand reverently over the bonnet's smooth surface.

'I can't hope to match it.' She stood, measurably overwhelmed as he brushed idle fingers down the length of her cheek.

'I don't expect you to.'

Sachi struggled with her emotions and lost miserably. 'Dominic——'

'I suggest we go inside.'

'Straight to the bedroom?' The words slipped out unintentionally, and she felt stricken at their implication.

'You imagine I'll demand sexual favours in return for such an expensive gift?' Dominic enquired silkily, his expression assuming a hard unfathomable mask.

'I didn't mean that the way it sounded,' she whispered, helpless in the face of such a damning turn of phrase.

'In that case, I would recommend you give some thought to your choice of words.'

For some inexplicable reason it hurt unbearably to have him doubt her, yet to continue to protest would only compound the situation.

A faint shiver shook her slight frame as she preceded him from the garage, and indoors, she made her way towards the central staircase, aware to a heightening degree of his presence as they reached their own private suite.

'You look incredibly—defenceless,' Dominic drawled as he closed the door behind them.

Slowly Sachi lifted her head and met his gaze. 'Perhaps it's because I am.'

He crossed the room towards her with an indolent ease.

'Against me?'

He was far too close, and she nervously swallowed the sudden lump that had risen in her throat. 'Yes.'

One eyebrow slanted with sardonic humour. 'That's quite an admission. Would you care to be more specific?'

No! a silent voice screamed from within. 'I feel as if I've unwittingly entered an unknown lair,' she said shakily, and saw his mouth twist to form a cynical smile.

'Which particular beast am I?'

'A tiger,' Sachi declared without hesitation.

'Should I be amused or insulted by the comparison?' he ruminated tolerantly as he shaped her face with his hands, tilting it so she had no chance of eluding his brooding gaze.

'Oh—*amused*. You haven't harmed so much as a hair on my head.'

'Disappointed, Sachi? Would you prefer a rough, more careless hand in bed?'

Her eyes became enmeshed with his, and she couldn't tear them away. 'No,' she answered with fearless honesty. I just want you to *love* me—to be your most precious possession. Yet such thoughts were bound in hopeless dreams, and she slowly veiled her eyes with a downward sweep of long thick lashes, afraid he might see through the windows of her mind to the depths of her very soul.

She felt the light brush of his lips against her temple, then he released her and shrugged off the jacket of his immaculate evening suit.

'Brent will be down for the weekend. He has only one more exam to sit before the end of term, and the break away from studies will help him unwind.'

Sachi viewed the prospect of entertaining his younger brother with mixed emotions, for it meant acting out a charade.

Slowly she undressed, handling her gown with care before crossing into the en suite to remove her make-up. In bed she lay still, waiting for the moment Dominic would pull her into his arms, and when he didn't she closed her eyes, unsure whether to be disappointed or thankful for the reprieve.

Dinner the following evening should have been a pleasant meal, for Janet had utilised her culinary skills to the utmost by preparing a chicken consommé, followed by veal escalopes in a delicate sauce accompanied by potatoes duchesse, beans garnished with sautéd onion and bacon, together with honeyed carrots sprinkled with sesame seeds. Dessert was an apple strudel served with clotted cream.

However, Sachi merely picked at each course, hardly tasting the excellent food, and her attempts at conversation could only be described as desultory at best.

'Is something bothering you?'

Dominic's drawled query was accompanied by a dark penetrating glance over coffee at the end of the meal.

What was the point in prevaricating? 'I received a cable this morning from Simone,' she enlightened without preamble, and saw his eyes narrow.

'Perhaps you'd care to tell me what it said?' He lifted his cup and took a generous sip of the aromatic brew, then replaced it on the saucer before leaning well back in his chair, the epitome of male sophistication and so damned indomitable she could have screamed with vexation.

It was years since she'd seen or even spoken to her sister. How could she explain her own confusion, torn as she was between a bond she knew didn't exist and the desperate need to believe Simone couldn't possibly pose a threat of any kind?

'She arrives in Sydney tomorrow, and intends catching a connecting flight to Brisbane. She'll ring me from her hotel as soon as she's settled in.'

Dominic's eyes lanced hers, analytically assessing in a way that made her want to pick up something and throw it at him.

'I imagine she'll want to see you.' The words slipped out unbidden, and she cursed herself for allowing old memories to surface.

'Perhaps you'd better explain precisely what you mean by that comment.' His tone was inflexible, his expression ruthless, and she shivered.

'Really, Dominic! I might have been a child, but I wasn't *blind*!'

There was a measured silence as he picked up his cup and drained its remaining contents. 'Aren't you being overly melodramatic?'

Sachi closed her eyes against the compelling sight of him, then slowly opened them again. '*No*, damn you! I'm not!' After all these years she could still *see* Dominic kissing Simone in the rear of the garden shed, and even now it hurt more than she would have believed possible.

His expression hardened, and his voice became a deep taunting drawl. 'Elaborate, Sachi.'

'I haven't a hope in hell against you,' she said bitterly. 'With mere words, or in an ability to match your physical strength.' To her utter consternation she felt the prick of tears behind her eyes, and the necessity to get out of the room and away from him was paramount.

With more haste than care she slid out of her chair and fled, except that she hadn't covered more than a few feet before strong hands caught and held her, then lifted her effortlessly over one shoulder.

'Put me down!' She beat her fists against his back and struggled with little effect. *'Bastard!'* Tears streamed from her eyes, dampening her hair. 'I hate you!'

All the way up the stairs she berated him, and even the faintly ominous sound of their bedroom door being kicked shut did little to stem the furious flow of words that flew from her mouth.

'Let me *go*, damn you!'

Dominic let her slide to the floor without a word, holding her flailing fists with galling ease.

'Oh, why are you doing this,' she cried, her breathing ragged as she glared at him. 'Leave me alone!'

The instant her hands were free she lashed out at him, balling her hands to hit his chest, his ribs—anywhere she could connect, until he caught them again in a merciless grip.

He regarded her assessingly, witnessing her heated cheeks, the storminess apparent in her eyes as he moved close. Taking hold of her chin, he lifted it, then his mouth lowered down over hers with bruising force, his invading tongue pillaging and destructive until she moaned a silent entreaty for him to desist.

With an angry gesture he pushed her to arm's length, and she swayed slightly as her knees began to buckle beneath her.

A husky oath caught her ears, and she winced against its explosive explicitness.

Dear God, what had she invited? Her lips felt swollen and sore, the soft inner tissue grazed. She was breaking up inside, every nerve stretched to its furthest limitation, and she cried out as he drew her towards him.

For a wild moment she thought Dominic meant to seek further retribution, and she actually flinched as his mouth sought hers in a kiss that was evocatively sensual.

With slow deliberation he brought alive every pulsing nerve-centre, dispensing with her clothes as easily as he shrugged off his own, then she gave a soundless gasp as his lips trailed a tantalising path down to her breast.

A faint moan escaped her lips as he scooped her into his arms and deposited her on the bed, powerless beneath an onslaught of emotion so treacherous she hadn't the willpower to resist his plundering lips as he deliberately circled one sensitive, tautened peak with his tongue, then drew it into his mouth to create a havoc so evocative that she actually shuddered, beseeching him with a series of guttural pleas he merely ignored as he moved to render a similar treatment to its twin.

Just when she thought she could stand it no longer, his mouth slid down to her waist, then trailed an erotic pattern to seek an impossible liberty, and she twisted beneath him, half crazed with the need for release.

'Damn you, Dominic,' she wept in frustration. 'Damn you to hell!'

He moved above her, meeting her silent demand for his possession, pacing her pleasure with his own until she soared high towards hitherto unreached heights, and for an all too brief moment she thought he almost lost control.

Although afterwards, as she lay supine and totally satiated, she decided she must have imagined it. She ached all over, her sensitised flesh alive in a way she wouldn't have thought possible after the physical torment created by his excessive demands.

And Dominic knew, his gaze warm with indolent amusement as he gently pulled her into his arms. The touch of his lips tantalised her own, their fleeting softness tracing the outline of her mouth before making slow, gentle forays to savour the moist sweetness inside.

Sachi's eyes widened slightly as she took in his vital, vibrant features, and she felt her lips tremble, unable to hide the haunting vulnerability evident before her eyes slid away from his.

With considerable care she slid to the edge of the bed, unaware that Dominic followed her into the en suite, where, despite her protestations, he gently pushed her into the shower cubicle and joined her beneath the jet of warm water.

Taking the soap, he cleansed her skin, then, placing her hand over his, he soaped his own body, his eyes never leaving hers, and she became filled with a treacherous weakness, wanting to smile and weep at the same time, yet too enervated to do anything other than suffer his ministrations.

It was only afterwards as she lay at his side close to sleep that she realised he had succeeded in placing her in a gilded prison. There were no bars to hold her, except those of her own making, irretrievably binding her to him in both soul and spirit, making any thought of escape impossible.

*   *   *

Sachi woke next morning with a terrible sense of foreboding, which was ridiculous, she decided as she forced herself to eat a nourishing breakfast.

The workmen arrived at eight o'clock and completed the finishing touches to the sitting-room adjoining the master bedroom, and two hours later a delivery van pulled into the driveway with the furniture she had ordered. By midday the room was complete, and resembled precisely her envisaged concept.

In a desperate bid to alleviate an increasing nervous tension Sachi suggested she aid Janet's culinary talents by assisting with dinner preparations. She became so engrossed that when the telephone rang mid-afternoon it took all of five seconds before she registered Janet's summons that the call was for her.

'Sachi, how are you?' The breath caught in her throat at the sound of that faintly husky, musical voice, and she felt a rush of nervous tension. 'Sachi? For heaven's sake, darling—it's *Simone*!' A tinkle of laughter accompanied the words.

'Simone.' Dear heaven, she had to get a hold on herself! 'How are you?'

'I know it's been fifteen years, darling. But *really*! It's not as if I haven't kept in touch.'

A few sketchy letters, a postcard or two, a card at Christmas. And nothing for Sam. Sachi's grip on the receiver tightened until the knuckles showed white. 'How was your flight?' she asked.

'Oh, *boring*. Air travel invariably *is*. Surely you remember?'

A long time ago, and then she'd been very young and consumed with childish excitement. 'Have you settled in OK?' If she didn't return to the present, she'd never manage to cope.

'Of course, darling.' There was a breathy laugh that seemed to strike a raw nerve, followed by an imperceptible pause that somehow dragged on a fraction too long.

Sachi closed her eyes, tightly, then slowly opened them. 'Perhaps we could meet for lunch?'

'Why, lunch will be fine. When, Sachi?'

Cautiously she ventured, 'Tomorrow?' There seemed no advantage in postponing the inevitable. 'Tell me where you're staying, and I'll meet you in the hotel foyer at one.'

Simone named one of the city's most exclusive hotels. 'Look forward to it, darling. *Ciao.*'

Sachi replaced the receiver with nerveless fingers, then walked quickly upstairs. She had half an hour before Dominic was due home, and she needed to change.

A shower cooled her skin, and after completing her toilette she slid into a wrap, then set about blowdrying her hair.

Selecting something to wear hardly posed a problem, and she chose a pale blue voile ensemble with splashes of lilac outlined in silver, matched it with fashionable silver high-heeled sandals, then went into the en suite to apply her make-up, restricting it to a touch of eyeliner and mascara and pale gloss on her lips.

'Enchanting!'

Sachi glanced up at the sound of that low-pitched drawl, and felt her pulse leap as it took on a quickened beat.

Dominic's eyes narrowed faintly as they conducted a leisurely appraisal of her outwardly composed features, and she forced her voice into level tones.

'Thank you.' The temptation to remain icily angry after last night was almost impossible to ignore. Except that he was an immovable force, and far more practised than she in a war of words. 'Will it suit you to have dinner in fifteen minutes? Janet and I collaborated to produce moussaka.'

Dominic shrugged off his suit jacket and loosened his tie. 'Give me time to change, then we'll have a drink and you can tell me about your day.' His eyes were strangely watchful above the lazy smile, and she tore her gaze away from the firm curve of his mouth.

'I'll check the oven.'

He let her escape, and downstairs in the kitchen her movements were entirely mechanical as she double-checked the oven's warming temperature and the contents of various serving dishes. Five minutes later she took a deep breath and made her way towards the lounge.

Dominic stood beside the carved rosewood cabinet, drink in hand, and Sachi forced herself to hold his gaze as she crossed the room to his side.

'A light wine, or something stronger?'

'Stronger.' Dammit, why should she *pretend*!

'Such as?'

Hell, he was so darned *cool*—invincible. Although, having witnessed his biting anger and been totally devastated by it, she far preferred this controlled façade.

'Brandy,' she said without the slightest qualm. 'With a dash of lime and lemonade.'

He shot her a wry smile. 'That bad? Perhaps you'd better tell me.'

There was nothing like the truth. 'Simone rang this afternoon.'

He mixed her drink and handed her the glass. 'And?'

'Just—*and*, Dominic?' It was hard to hold on to her temper, but she managed—barely. She took a tentative sip from her glass, then followed it with another, feeling the strength of the diluted brandy as it hit her empty stomach. Careful, a tiny imp warned. You need courage, not anger—and neither will be much help encumbered by a mist of alcohol. Her chin tilted fractionally as she looked at him with an equanimity she was far from feeling.

'I'm meeting her for lunch tomorrow.'

Dominic took a leisurely swallow, then paused to regard the remaining contents of his tumbler before subjecting her to an objective appraisal.

'Would you like me to join you?'

'In the guise of my protector, Dominic?'

The words were torn from her lips in anguished query, and his eyes assumed a frightening inflexibility.

'Is that what you think?'

Sachi didn't know what to think any more. She only knew it was becoming increasingly impossible to separate the intensity of their lovemaking and isolate it in her mind from her own insecurities.

'In case you haven't noticed, I'm all grown up,' she said bitterly. 'I don't need you to protect me from anyone. Not even Simone,' she concluded, hiding an incredible sadness as she escaped into the kitchen to serve dinner, and afterwards she was immeasurably relieved when Dominic retired into the study on the premise of work.

CHAPTER NINE

SACHI discarded one outfit after another in her quest for a garment portraying sophistication to wear for her luncheon date with Simone, and after much agonising she opted for a multi-coloured Diane Freis designer frock. Its soft easy-care fabric was totally feminine, and she matched it with red high-heeled shoes and clutch purse. Make-up was applied with care, and at twelve-thirty she stood back from the mirror, pleased with her overall image.

The hotel where they were to meet was situated in the inner city, and Sachi entered its foyer at precisely one o'clock.

'Sachi!' a sultry voice greeted her, and she turned at once, a rather nervous smile parting her mouth.

Quite what she expected after all these years she wasn't sure, but the woman who stood before her looked no more than thirty and was perfection personified in an elegant black suit with black and white accessories.

'Simone! How are you?'

'Oh, *fine*,' Simone answered with a brilliant smile. 'Shall we go into the restaurant?'

Seated at a table, Simone proceeded to order champagne, a bottle of Cristal, which she declared was the only fitting tribute to their reunion.

'Now, darling,' she began as soon as the waiter had served their starter, 'I'm avidly curious to know how you came to marry Dominic.' She carefully studied her beautifully manicured nails. 'A little too much of a coincidence for it to be *love*, wouldn't you say?'

Oh, dear lord, this held the threat of digressing rapidly into bitterness. 'Dominic asked me to marry him, Simone,' Sachi relayed quietly. 'Not the other way round.'

'Yes, darling. But have you ever given a thought as to why?'

Sachi picked at the contents on her plate, then pushed it to one side, her appetite gone as the nerves inside her stomach played havoc with her digestive system. In the need to change the subject, she clutched at the first thing that came to mind. 'I was sorry to hear about your divorce.'

'Don't be, darling. I'm not.'

The waiter removed their plates and served the main course, while the wine steward took care to refill Simone's glass.

'I understand Dominic has completely restored the house,' Simone ventured with purposeful interest. 'It's quite a showplace, I believe.'

It was more than that—much more. 'It's beautiful,' Sachi acknowledged simply, and saw her sister's eyes harden.

Simone lifted the flute to her perfectly outlined mouth and sipped a generous measure of champagne. 'A little advice, darling. Don't regard your newfound status with too much permanence.'

Sachi met her sister's glittery gaze with innate dignity. 'I learnt a long time ago never to take *anything* for granted.'

'I imagine you're very much into the social scene? It must make for quite a change after years of playing nursemaid.'

She closed her eyes tightly, then slowly opened them, determined to maintain control. 'I have few aspirations to be a social butterfly, and I intend to continue with my job,' she revealed drily.

'Good heavens. You still *work*?' Simone queried with veiled amusement. 'One can only wonder at Dominic's reaction.'

'He accepts that I want to continue my career.'

'Doing what, darling? Selling furniture?'

What could they pursue as a conversational topic after more than fifteen years' absence? Sachi wondered with a certain sadness. It would take a miracle for Simone to have become the type of sister with whom she could form an affectionate bond.

The waiter served their coffee, and when the bill was presented Simone carelessly pushed it across the table.

'Yours, I think. Dominic can certainly afford it.'

Sachi tendered a credit card in payment, then followed Simone out into the hotel foyer.

'How long do you intend staying in Brisbane?' she asked.

'It all depends. We will, of course, see each other again soon.' Simone leant forward and touched Sachi's cheek. *'Ciao.'*

The luncheon had been, Sachi decided as she drove home, a lesson in abject futility. Simone hadn't changed at all, and still remained the self-orientated, totally selfish girl Sachi remembered from her youth.

Perhaps it was as well Brent was due this evening to stay the weekend. At least his company should provide some light relief, and the ensuing two days might even prove to be fun.

Much to Sachi's delight, her expectations turned out to be correct, for she discovered in Brent a mutual empathy for music and art. Together with Dominic, they played tennis after dinner, then cooled off in the pool for a while before retreating indoors to shower and change.

Dominic appeared totally relaxed, even faintly amused by his brother's flirtatious banter and Sachi's spontaneous response as they opposed each other in a game of billiards, and it was after midnight before they all retired to bed.

The following day was spent sailing on Moreton Bay, and in retrospect, Sachi couldn't remember feeling so completely relaxed as she shared both men's company.

Her eyes glowed with genuine enjoyment as she put the finishing touches to her make-up in preparation for a party they were to attend that evening in the home of one of Dominic's associates to celebrate the hosts' daughter's graduation.

'You look stunning,' Dominic told her in approval of her white designer-label gown as she moved into the bedroom and collected her evening purse.

'Why, thank you.' An impish smile tugged the edges of her mouth. 'You look decidedly handsome yourself.'

Attired in a black dinner suit, a stark white shirt and bow tie, he looked every inch the wealthy executive, urbane, sophisticated, and exuding raw masculinity from every nerve and fibre.

Sachi wanted to walk up to him and have his arms close around her, to pull his head down to hers for the kind of kiss that held a promise of how the night would end. Except she didn't quite possess the courage.

Something flared in the depths of his eyes for a few heartstopping seconds, almost as if he had read her thoughts, then it was gone.

'Ready?' he asked.

The party, held in a splendid home in neighbouring Ascot, was an enormous success, with sufficient vintage champagne and gourmet food to satisfy the most critical guest.

It was quite late when Sachi heard a soft feminine, hauntingly familiar voice close by, and she turned slowly to see Simone in a clinging black creation on the arm of a distinguished-looking man.

Her heart plummeted, and it took considerable effort to voice a seemingly affectionate greeting.

'Simone! How nice to see you.'

'Yes, darling, isn't it?' Simone's brilliant eyes flashed, then became veiled as she introduced her companion. 'How remiss of Dominic to leave you on your own!'

'I was just about to rejoin him,' Sachi informed her, offering a slight smile.

'He doesn't appear to have noticed your absence.'

The words stung, and there seemed little point in revealing that she had only left Dominic's side minutes before to visit the powder-room. With a brief inclination of her head she excused herself and began threading her way across the room.

'What's the problem?'

Sachi glanced towards the attractive young man who appeared at her side as if by magic, and she barely succeeded in stifling the hollow laugh that threatened to choke in her throat. 'What makes you think I have one?'

'My dear sister-in-law,' Brent chided gently, 'let the record show that I think you're the best thing that ever happened to my awesome brother. In fact,' he declared with mock-seriousness, 'if he hadn't whipped you off to the nearest church in record time to make it legal, I'd have no qualms about staking a claim myself.'

'Ah—flattery,' Sachi teased with a genuinely warm smile.

'You don't believe me?'

'You're great fun,' she said gently. 'And I really enjoy your company.'

'But you belong to Dominic.' His solemn dark eyes held a mischievous twinkle. 'I'll have you know I'm nursing a broken heart.'

'Which I'm sure one of at least three girls present tonight will attempt to mend, given the slightest hint of interest from you,' Sachi declared with ill-disguised laughter, then sobered quickly as he caught hold of her hand and lifted it to his lips in a gesture that was endearing and old-fashionedly gallant.

'Compared to you, they're girlish and giggly and incredibly boring.'

'I think you'd better stop playing the fool,' she admonished quietly. 'Dominic has just directed us the most riveting glance.'

'We could make him jealous,' suggested Brent as he relinquished her hand with obvious reluctance. 'Then again, perhaps not. He governs the purse-strings to my allowance, and incurring his anger wouldn't be advisable. Now,' he directed, giving her a totally disarming grin, 'tell me what's bothering you.'

A generous smile curved her lips, lightening her eyes to a clear sparkling gold. 'You're impossible, do you know that?'

'Oh, so they all tell me. It's just a façade. Underneath it all, I'm a model of sobriety, a serious medical student who gains straight "A"s and has written accolades from numerous professors to prove it. I hope sheer brilliance in my chosen specialised field will confound you in another decade.' The veneer of tomfoolery was remarkably absent. 'But for now, all this light banter is temporary madness—a relief from heavy lectures and long hours of serious study.' A gleam of humour returned, together with a winsome, totally charming smile. 'I happen to think you're gorgeous, and I really need to know the reason for that funny, sad little shadow lurking in the depths of those beautiful eyes.'

'Psychology, or psychiatry?' queried Sachi. 'It just has to be one or the other.'

'Same area, wrong field. Neuro-surgery,' he responded with light mockery. 'And don't change the subject.'

'You must know I can't discuss it.'

'Ah—*loyalty*!' Brent glimpsed the faint trembling of her lips, and his own tightened infinitesimally. 'Well, darling, if it's worth anything, Dominic is a giant among men. I say that entirely without prejudice.' He took her glass and put it with his own on a nearby table. 'Now, let's kick up our heels and dance. Not exactly my kind of music, but I guess I can bear with it.'

He was engaging and extremely kind. Sachi told him so as he took her in his arms on the dance-floor, and he returned the compliment, whispering the words in her ear with such overt conspiracy that she found it impossible not to smile.

If only she shared a similar affinity with his elder brother! Her wayward thoughts trailed off to a halt as she caught sight of Dominic engaged in conversation with Simone. Correction, they were each part of a mingling group, and although Simone's features were vividly alive, Dominic's expression could only be described as attentively polite.

At that precise moment he glanced up and caught Sachi's gaze, and she sent him an incredibly dazzling smile. Simone caught it too, and she lifted scarlet-tipped nails to touch Dominic's sleeve, her lips forming a faint moue in supposed commiseration as Brent whirled Sachi between fellow dancers with dashing flair.

'I think we're being observed,' Sachi chided a trifle breathlessly as Brent caught her close in recognition of the changed tempo of music.

'Dominic would trust me with your life,' he declared lightly. 'Besides, he's deep in conversation with two fellow barristers and their wives. These social occasions are merely a disguise for the eminent few to talk shop. He drew back a fraction and offered a beguiling smile. 'Wouldn't you prefer to dance with me than be forced to listen politely to *jurisprudence*?'

'Ten years down the track, when you're a noted neuro-surgeon, and you attend one of these numerous social functions,' she posed solemnly, 'will you prefer your wife at your side, or frivolously dancing with someone else?'

'Frivolously?' He grinned in total unrepentance. 'I am the total gentleman. However,' he added quietly, 'point taken. Shall I escort you back?'

'I was just about to suggest the same thing,' Dominic drawled from behind, and Sachi faltered and missed her step as a *frisson* of apprehension shivered across the surface of her skin.

'Your precious possession.' Brent surrendered her into his brother's arms before threading his way through the crowd.

Sachi felt she should say something, but nothing appropriate came immediately to mind, and she made no protest as Dominic drew her close. So close, her body appeared welded to his from her thigh to the tip of her head in a far from conventional grasp.

In tune to the low-tempo music their bodies moved as one, with perfect fluidity, and she shifted her head slightly in the curve of his shoulder, unaware of the faint sigh that whispered from her lips.

This was heaven, the one place she wanted— *needed* to be. In the arms of the man she loved.

The revelation shocked her, for although she'd been loath to analyse her feelings, not once had she ever considered them as anything remotely resembling love. Physical desire had become a mesmeric sensual pleasure so exquisite she could hardly breathe—a sensation she had innocently interpreted as resulting from Dominic's sexual expertise.

Yet it was more than that, much more. He had become her reason for living—her whole existence.

Somehow the rest of the evening retained a distinct blur as she danced with Dominic, then alternately stood by his side, listening, participating in conversation with more than impartial interest, all the while aware of him with an intensity that was vaguely frightening.

Could he sense it? she wondered, leaning back against the car's soft leather cushioning as he sent the vehicle purring through the busy city streets.

Sachi closed her eyes as her mind dwelled on Simone and her unannounced presence at the graduation party. Her sister's precise purpose was unclear, although there was every possibility that Simone might consider it amusing to create some form of mischief.

It was almost three when the car drew to a halt inside the garage, and Sachi followed Dominic indoors, her emotions held tightly in control as she made her way upstairs to their room.

A strange tingling sensation raced through her veins, and even her breathing was behaving in an erratic fashion as she ignored the light-switch and crossed to the window.

The sky held the darkness of velvet, the distant stars seeming to possess a distinct similarity to the delicate tracery of street lights stretching far out towards the horizon. It looked so peaceful, yet beneath that deceptively calm mantle lay the isolated violence of a modern night-time city, and Sachi shivered slightly.

'Cold?'

Sachi shook her head, and felt all her fine body hairs stand erect in shocking awareness of Dominic's presence as his arms slid round her waist from behind. His breath was warm against her temple, teasing a few stray tendrils of hair as he drew her back against him, and a shaft of exquisite pleasure exploded deep within as his mouth moved down to settle on the delicate curve of her nape.

She should tell him to stop, yet she was spellbound by the depth of her own emotions and powerless to prevent the light caressing touch of his hand as it slid over her ribcage to capture her breast.

His tongue became an erotic instrument as he traced the delicate hollows at the edge of her neck, savouring the throbbing pulse before gently trailing the sensitive cord to tease her earlobe with tantalising deliberation.

To consider fighting him was impossible, for to push him away meant a denial of sensual ecstasy so acute it was all she could do not to beg for assuagement, and a small sigh escaped her lips as she gave in to the witching arousal of the senses, exulting in the slow rapturous stimulation until a fierce hunger arose, demanding release.

She became a willing supplicant, helping him discard first her clothes, then his own, and she clung to him unashamedly as their lovemaking assumed a wild, passionate quality that became a total ravishment, the joy of two spirits in perfect accord.

Afterwards she slept, her body imprisoned within the possessive shelter of his arms, and there were no dark demons chasing her dreams, no elusive sadness to mar the sheer beauty of their consummation.

They rose late the next morning, ate a lazy breakfast of fruit and cereal on the terrace, then drove down to the Coast for what remained of the day, enjoyed a barbecue at one of the many resorts, and returned to Brisbane long after dark.

Brent regretfully declined to stay overnight, preferring instead to drive back to the flat he shared near the medical school, and soon after he left Sachi made her way upstairs to bed. She was more tired than she cared to admit, and besides, tomorrow she would resume work at Poissant.

*   *   *

During the following few days life settled back into a busy pattern, with Sachi leaving the house each morning within minutes of Dominic, and returning at three each afternoon. The hours suited her admirably, for it meant she had time to relax before Dominic arrived home.

Of Simone there had been no word, and Sachi couldn't help feeling vaguely uneasy, torn between a sense of duty to place a phone call to the hotel and an innate reluctance to do so.

Thursday was remarkably quiet—so much so that Henri Poissant suggested she finish at midday and take advantage of the extra few hours in which to do some Christmas shopping. Except that Sachi felt more inclined to spend a few hours relaxing by the pool at home than jostling fellow shoppers in the city.

Consequently it was almost one when she arrived home, just in time to check dinner arrangements with Janet before the housekeeper left to drop Tom at the nearby garage to collect Dominic's Mercedes from its routine service check.

'I'll go on to the supermarket and do the shopping,' Janet advised as she went out of the door. 'I should be back about three.'

Sachi made her way upstairs and changed her clothes for something infinitely more casual, then she collected a glass of fruit juice from the refrigerator, picked up a magazine and went out to sit by the pool.

A short while later the sound of electronic chimes echoed through the house, and she sped indoors, curious to know who could be calling at this time of day.

'Simone!' It was almost impossible to disguise the shocked surprise in her voice as she stood back from the open door.

'Good heavens, Sachi,' her sister reproved with a delicately arched brow, 'aren't you going to at least invite me in?'

'Of course.' Why should she suddenly feel wary and vaguely apprehensive? 'Would you prefer the lounge, or outside by the pool?'

'Oh, the lounge. I'd love a drink—preferably something long and cool.' Simone turned midway through the foyer. 'Are you alone?'

'Yes.' Somehow the admission made Sachi feel incredibly vulnerable. 'I haven't long arrived home from work.'

Simone's attention was taken by the redecoration apparent as they entered the lounge. 'Dominic has certainly expended a fortune.'

Sachi refrained from commenting on the obvious as she crossed to the drinks cabinet. 'Anything in particular, Simone?'

'Gin and ice, with a squeeze of lime, a dash of bitters, and lemonade.'

Sachi poured the requisite mixture, then handed her sister the chilled glass.

'Cheers, darling. To happy memories.'

'Past or future?' queried Sachi.

'Oh, *future*, darling,' Simone declared in tinkling tones. 'You can't honestly believe this—*arranged* marriage of yours can possibly *last*?' She leaned forward, her features assuming incredible pity. 'You haven't a hope of holding a man like Dominic. He needs a *woman* in his bed, well versed in the art of seduction and able to satisfy his every demand. Not some inhibited young thing who would draw the line at sensual titillation.'

'You're disgusting!' Sachi was sickened by Simone's implication, and suffered the force of her sister's pitiless laughter.

'Dear God, Sachi, how can you be so naïve? I suppose *you* went to the altar as a virgin bride.'

'I'd like you to leave,' Sachi said dully, aware that the only way this invective could go was down.

Simone had timed her call well. Never before had Sachi been aware of being so defencelessly alone.

'No,' Simone refused, extending a manicured finger to flick Sachi's cheek with a lightness that held an underlying hint of malice. 'You really have blossomed into quite an attractive little girl. My last memory of you was of a rather gawky young child with long plaits and braces.' Her eyes raked Sachi's apparel with scathing disregard. 'For the wife of an extremely rich man, you're a little slow on the uptake, aren't you, darling?' she said archly and uncharitably. 'I've noticed a few pieces of acceptable jewellery, but nothing spectacular. And your clothes—well, they're hardly products of the designer élite. In Dominic's position, he can afford to let you spend a fortune.'

'I don't see the need to wear glamour gear for a quiet afternoon at home,' Sachi said quietly, wondering why she was bothering to defend the neatly tailored shorts she wore with a contrasting sleeveless top.

Simone took time to examine her nails, then speared her sister with a glittery glance. 'I find the image you both present extremely interesting, and almost impossible to fault. The light touch of the hand, the intimate glance whenever anyone else is around.' She paused imperceptibly. 'I'm curious to know what it's like when you're alone.'

Sachi chose her words carefully. 'We're very fond of each other.'

Both eyebrows rose in supercilious cynicism. *'Fond?'* Her laughter was slightly off key. 'You're merely a convenient appendage! Can't you see that?' Simone's eyes held a malevolent gleam. 'And a *Tarrant*! It's common knowledge that Father gambled himself into poverty. How Dominic must be laughing at his two-fold revenge—not only has he bought and restored the property, he's installed one of Simon Tarrant's daughters as his wife! You'd have to be incredibly stupid not to recognise that your marriage is a constant source of speculation among the social élite.' A look of pure enmity consumed her features. 'He doesn't love *you*, darling.'

Quietly Sachi stood her ground, her gaze unwavering as she tried to judge the limit of Simone's control, defensive yet curiously alert for any unprecedented action as she crossed to the phone and punched out the required digits, then voiced the necessary request before replacing the receiver.

'A taxi will take you back to your hotel. There seems little point in continuing this conversation.'

Despite the extent of her sister's resentment, Sachi was unprepared for the rage that erupted in the form of vitriolic invective, accompanied by a painful slap to her left cheek, so viciously hard that it knocked her sideways to the floor.

Shocked almost beyond comprehension, she cried out as the toe of Simone's shoe connected with her ribs. She dimly registered a stern voice in the background at the same time as her sister's screaming subsided into a defensive whimper, then strong hands lifted her into a nearby chair, and Tom's kindly expression entered her peripheral vision, welcome and incredibly reassuring.

Within minutes Simone was escorted from the house and put into a waiting taxi, and during that time Sachi leaned back in the chair, her features frozen into an expressionless mask as the outcome of her sister's unexpected visit reverberated with shattering clarity through her mind.

'I'm fine—really,' she assured Tom as he re-entered the lounge, and knew it to be a lie. Her eyes felt incredibly large, and her head throbbed, so much so that even the slightest breath caused incredible distress.

In silence she watched Tom pick up the phone, and his voice was concise as he rang the doctor, then the office requesting Nicole to despatch an urgent message to Dominic.

It was useless to protest that she didn't need medical attention, and equally impossible to suggest that Dominic should be kept in ignorance.

With curious detachment Sachi sipped the hot sweet tea Tom brought, and upon Janet's arrival she attempted to stem the threat of tears, for although that good woman was sufficiently diplomatic not to pass comment, one glance at her sympathetic features was enough to heighten Sachi's vulnerability to a point where it became almost impossible to retain control.

Dominic's appearance within minutes of the doctor's departure merely strengthened her resolve not to disintegrate into a trembling mess.

'I've heard Tom's version of what happened,' Dominic began quietly. 'Perhaps you'd care to fill in the missing details.'

One glance at his expression was enough to send a chill shiver through her veins, and she lifted a hand to her hair in a strangely defensive gesture.

In a halting voice she told him, aware that his eyes never left hers for an instant, and when she had finished he gently lifted her top to inspect the inflamed swelling covering two of her ribs.

'Why not go upstairs to bed?'

'Good heavens, whatever for? I'm not ill.'

'Indulge me.' His features softened, although his eyes resembled hard obsidian chips. 'I have to make a phone call.'

She knew before she asked, but she couldn't prevent the query, 'To Simone?'

His mouth tightened with frightening severity. 'Informing her that if she isn't on a plane out of Brisbane within twenty-four hours, she'll be called upon to answer charges of assault with intent to cause bodily harm.'

Sachi could only look at him in electrifying silence. 'Is that really necessary?'

'Yes,' Dominic drawled irrefutably, then he leant forward and brushed his lips across her forehead. 'Janet will bring up a tray with something light for you to eat. I'll check on you later.'

I don't need you to check on me! Sachi felt like screaming, except that the sedative the doctor had given her removed the impetus for anger, and she merely nodded her head in silent acquiescence. One scene was sufficient. She doubted she could cope with another.

Within minutes of slipping into bed she felt her eyelids flutter down, and she didn't attempt to fight the lethargy creeping slowly throughout her entire body.

Sachi stirred at some stage through the night, unaware for a few disorientated seconds what had disturbed her sleep. Then she felt the mattress depress slightly as Dominic slid quietly into bed beside her, and she tensed, alternately needing the warm security of his arms, and wanting to be left alone.

However, he made no move towards her, and she lay still for what seemed an age before the sound of his breathing slowed to a deep, steady rhythm.

It should have been easy to slip back into a dreamless state, but instead she became plagued by Simone's viciousness, both verbal and physical, creating a mental agony that had nothing to do with bodily pain.

The inability to sleep finally prompted her to slip out of bed, and sliding her arms into a silken wrap she made her way towards the bathroom further down the hall in the hope that a nice hot bath might prove a soothing balm to her shattered nerves.

On impulse she added delicately perfumed oil which created a layer of bubbles, then she pinned up her hair and stepped into the deliciously warm water.

Relax, she silently bade her body. Just relax and don't think. But as much as she tried, Simone's image rose up to taunt her, and it was impossible not to relive the afternoon's terrible scene.

'So this is where you are,' a deep voice drawled from the open doorway, and her eyes widened measurably as they flew to meet his, their depths mirroring innate fragility for one brief second before her lashes swept down to form a protective shield.

Beneath the fringed lashes she saw him cross the room and sit down on the edge of the bath, and a thousand tiny nerve-endings leapt into pulsating life.

A hand reached out and warm fingers caught hold of her chin and lifted it so that she became trapped in his steadfast gaze.

'I couldn't sleep,' Sachi offered by way of explanation. There was a haunting, almost hunted quality apparent in her expression, and her mouth trembled beneath the light brush of his fingertips.

'I think it's time you came back to bed,' Dominic suggested gently. 'You've been out of it for half an hour.'

'You knew?'

He smiled, a slow, soft widening of his mouth that made her melt into a thousand pieces. 'Yes.' He leant forward and kissed her with such silken sweetness she became victim of a maelstrom of emotions, feelings that were too complex to distinguish any *one*, and she could only look at him as he reached out and released the bathplug.

Within seconds the tide of bubbles had diminished, and she stood to her feet, accepting the large bathtowel he held out, and it was only when he had gently dried her that she felt a treacherous ache behind her eyes. She blinked rapidly to dispel the threat of tears as he caught up her nightgown and slid it over her head.

'Don't cry,' Dominic bade softly, bending his head low to brush his lips against her temple. 'Simone flies back to the States tomorrow. The threat of pressed charges proved to be an extremely persuasive factor.'

Sachi couldn't find any words in response, and she made no protest as he slid an arm beneath her knees and carried her back to their bedroom.

'Please don't touch me,' she begged as he let her slip down to her feet beside the bed. The tears she had held at bay filled her eyes and spilled over to trickle slowly down each cheek. 'I don't think I could bear it.'

She swayed slightly, feeling incredibly threatened, and she could only watch in mesmerised fascination as he caught hold of her hand and buried his lips in her palm.

His eyes never left hers for a second as he drew the soft skin gently into his mouth, teasing with erotic sensitivity, and she felt an exquisite shaft of pleasure explode deep within.

It would be so easy to close her eyes and allow him to draw her into a vortex of sensual ecstasy. Except that no longer was enough.

'Whatever Simone alluded to has no basis in relation to the reason for our marriage,' Dominic insisted quietly.

She couldn't look at him, and she stood immobile as his hands slid up her arms to rest at her shoulders.

'I wanted *you*,' he declared gently. 'With your courage and dignity.' He lifted a hand to cup her chin, tilting it so that she had no recourse but to meet his gaze. 'Not because you were Sachi *Tarrant*.'

The faint huskiness in his voice did strange things to her equilibrium, and she stood transfixed by the deep, slumbrous ardency of his gaze. As if in a dream she lifted her arms and linked her hands together at his nape, loving the feel of his slightly ruffled hair as she slid her fingers through its groomed length, and she made no demur as his mouth lowered down to hers in a kiss that was so incredibly gentle she almost wanted to die from the need for him to deepen it.

Except he didn't, and she felt strangely bereft as he lifted her into bed and cradled her body against his own, his hands stroking soothingly over fragile bones, sensitising her flesh in a manner that made sleep impossible.

CHAPTER TEN

THE next few days were unbearable. Dominic was incredibly solicitous, Janet and Tom so kind, that between them all, Sachi felt as if she was being stifled to death.

By Sunday morning she was a mass of nerves, unsure of anything except a need to get away on her own for an unspecified period of time.

'You're extremely pensive,' Dominic drawled across the width of the breakfast table.

Her eyes were clear and direct as they met his, although her faint smile was a poor imitation. 'I need to be alone for a while.' There, she'd actually said it.

'Why not have a week at the Bayview Harbour apartment?'

'You would actually allow me to go?'

'If that's what you want.'

Want? Dear God, she dared not give voice to what she wanted! That was an impossible dream—a fantasy. And there was no place for fantasy in the reality of her life. Loving him had become a living hell, and her growing discontent with the *status quo* merely provided the need to examine every nuance in his voice, his expression, for some sign that his passion in bed wasn't born out of lust.

'I will go down to the Coast,' she declared with sudden resolve. 'I'll pack a few things and leave this afternoon.'

'Why not postpone it until tomorrow?'

It must be *now*. His lovemaking had a devastating effect on her equilibrium, and after spending another night in his arms she might easily be swayed into staying. Slowly she shook her head, her expressive features unusually grave. 'I'd rather get away as soon as possible. You have work to do on your brief for tomorrow's hearing.' She even managed a faint smile. 'You won't have time to miss me.'

There was a momentary darkness in the depths of Dominic's eyes, then it was gone, and he moved away from the window, his expression assuming detached inscrutability.

'I'll be in the study. Call in and collect the keys to the apartment before you leave.'

Without a further word Sachi turned and walked from the room, feeling as if her heart were tearing in two—which was a complete misconception, for hearts were sturdy organs and didn't tear, or break.

Upstairs in their suite, she flung clothes at random into a capacious holdall before crossing to the en suite to collect toiletries and cosmetics. Opting not to change out of shorts, she simply added a blouse over her sleeveless top, then she ran a mental check to ascertain if she'd forgotten anything before closing the zip fastening. Snatching up her shoulder-bag, she slung it over one shoulder, caught up the holdall, and without so much as a backward glance she walked from the room and ran lightly downstairs.

The study door was open, and Dominic glanced up as she came in. For a split second as he slipped off his reading glasses he looked incredibly weary, the fine lines etching his eyes seeming more pronounced, the grooves slashing his cheeks deeper.

As she crossed to the desk he stood to his feet and took the holdall from her grasp.

'I'll see you to the car.'

Sachi couldn't believe he was letting her go so easily, and she followed him out to the garage, to stand hesitantly unsure as he deposited her gear into the boot of the Honda Prelude. Even her smile was distinctly shaky as he dropped two sets of keys into her hand, and her nerves created a havoc all their own as he reached out and opened the door. Without thought she stood on tiptoe and brushed her lips against the edge of his jaw.

'Thanks,' she said awkwardly, feeling childish and incredibly gauche.

'If you're going to thank me,' he said with a touch of mockery, 'at least do it properly.' His eyes were unreadable, his smile slow and lazy as he caught hold of her shoulders.

Dear God, what was he trying to do to her? Demand some sort of penance? And it hurt unbearably that he was amused. 'Dominic—don't——'

'What?' The warmth of his body was a potent, virile force, and she felt herself sway towards him as if drawn by a powerful magnet. 'Tease,' she whispered in a strange breathless voice, knowing that *tease* was far too tame a description. Tormenting, *torturing*, were far more apt.

'Really, Sachi,' he chided gently, 'why display such reluctance? A kiss is no big deal, surely?'

It depended whether he intended a fleeting merging of their mouths, or something infinitely more evocative. For some reason she felt physically threatened, afraid that anything other than a transitory gesture would dissolve the tenuous hold she retained on her emotions, and she watched with a kind of stupefied fascination as his head lowered to hers, unaware that her lips parted involuntarily in mesmerised anticipation of his touch.

With feather-lightness he traced the outline of her mouth, lingering at one edge before brushing back to the other side, his tongue tasting the soft full curves as he gently savoured the inner sweetness, probing, possessing with such seductive warmth that it was all she could do not to cling to him in a manner that would issue its own invitation.

With unconscious volition her hands crept up to his shoulders, shaking slightly as they encompassed strong muscle and sinew beneath the light cotton of his shirt.

Dear lord in heaven, it would be so easy to stay— to persuade herself to be content with superficial emotions. Lust, a tiny voice taunted. There was little doubt Dominic found her physically attractive and desirable in bed. But any one out of a hundred a *thousand*—other women could fulfil that need. What reason was there for her to believe *she* might be sufficiently special to warrant his love?

With conscious effort she let her hands slip slowly down to rest against each muscular forearm, at the same time reluctantly relinquishing her mouth.

His eyes were dark with lambent warmth, and there was a sensuality apparent that brought a lump to her throat. To stand here was madness—yet she was powerless to move as he lifted a hand and idly traced his finger down the tapering length of her nose. When he brushed her temple in a gentle fleeting gesture she pulled away from him and turned blindly towards the car.

'Ring me as soon as you arrive,' Dominic drawled as she slid in behind the wheel.

He closed the door and she fired the engine, easing the car down the driveway towards the gate, then out on to the street.

Despite the warmth of the summer's afternoon the heat failed to penetrate the air-conditioned interior as she bypassed the inner city and connected with the F3 leading direct to the Coast.

The car flew beneath her competent hands, and it was only when she seemed to be passing every vehicle travelling on the inside lane that she spared the speedometer a glance and registered that her speed was far in excess of the legal limit. Immediately she eased back, then she reached for a tape and inserted it into the cassette deck in the hope that music might soothe her tense nerves.

Why did she feel so—*bereft*? Getting away from Dominic and everything he stood for was what she desperately wanted, wasn't it? Yet, conversely, she began to wonder if escaping was the answer, because eventually she would have to return. Unless she forced a resolution. A decision that was fraught with risk, for although the marriage was mutually convenient, she had everything to lose if it came to an end. And, if she was totally honest, she had grown accustomed to not having to worry about every cent—experiencing delight at indulging in shopping expeditions where price was no object. Was she being incredibly selfish to want her husband's love as well?

Dimly she registered the flashing signal of a highway patrol car, followed almost simultaneously by the wail of its siren, and she automatically moved into the inner lane to allow the vehicle free passage. Except that within seconds it became clear that *she* was the one they were chasing, and with a sinking feeling she brought her car to a halt on the highway's gravelled edge.

Damn, *damn*! she cursed beneath her breath as a uniformed officer approached, notebook in hand.

Five minutes and a sternly delivered lecture later, she was feeling suitably chastened and in possession of a speeding ticket which carried an excessive fine.

In a way it was a relief to pass through the entrance gates to Bayview Harbour and head towards Les Colonnades, where, with the car safely garaged, she activated the air-conditioning, re-set the security system, then headed through to the lounge.

It was a glorious day, and the marine berths were filled with pleasure craft of various sizes and descriptions, the afternoon sun reflecting against the smooth blue waters of the inner harbour.

There was an incredible sense of peace apparent in these surroundings, Sachi acknowledged gratefully, a tranquillity that had been deliberately sought by its developers. Successfully achieved, she credited with a faint sigh of contentment as she crossed to the telephone and punched out the necessary digits to connect her with Dominic.

'Sachi,' he greeted her on the second ring, indicating that he had picked up the call from the study. 'You made good time.'

'Almost too good,' she revealed with a faint grimace. 'I collected a ticket.'

There was a fractional silence, then he drawled, 'One hopes your speed wasn't too excessive.'

'About thirty kilometres over the limit,' she confessed, aware that there was no point in resorting to fabrication.

'Take care, my sweet wife.' There was a hint of steel in his voice that held, unless she was mistaken, a tinge of concern. 'I don't fancy you as another road accident statistic.'

'It wasn't intentional,' she reassured him at his warning chastisement.

'I don't imagine it was,' said Dominic drily.

If she didn't make an attempt at levity, they'd probably digress into dissension. 'No speeding tickets on your records, Dominic—ever?' she teased lightly. 'I seem to recollect you driving an aged but racy MGB.'

'Do me a favour, Sachi. Keep a gentle foot on the accelerator in future.'

'Yes, *sir*.' From this distance she could afford to be cheeky, and she heard his husky chuckle in response.

'I could always be persuaded into joining you for a well-deserved vacation. However, considering your expressed need to be alone...' His voice trailed to a deliberate halt, and the nerves in her stomach clenched in sudden pain.

'I promise to be a model of sobriety,' Sachi managed solemnly.

'Thank you.' The faint mockery in his voice merely served to hasten her need to end their conversation.

'I'll ring and let you know when I'm ready to return.' She replaced the receiver before he had the opportunity to pass comment, and stood staring pensively at the telephone, half expecting him to ring back with a qualifying rejoinder, except that he didn't, and after a few timeless minutes she moved away, collected her holdall and carried it through to the bedroom.

Unpacking was a simple chore which occupied only a few minutes, and afterwards she changed into a bikini and made her way out on to the patio.

Agonising over the degree, if any, of Dominic's emotional commitment would do no good at all. She had come here to relax in solitude, and that was precisely what she intended, she determined as she smoothed on sunscreen cream before stretching out on one of the loungers.

After an hour she went indoors to shower and shampoo her hair, then she slipped into shorts and a top, and went into the kitchen to inspect the contents of the pantry and the refrigerator-freezer.

An omelette with cheese, tomato and bacon filling, she decided, and a slice of bread, toasted, from a packet in the freezer would satisfactorily appease her hunger. Then after she'd eaten, she'd view television for a few hours, read for a while, then retire to bed.

Tomorrow she'd drive to Sanctuary Cove and browse among the boutiques, treat herself to lunch, and put her name down for a game of tennis on her return.

Which was precisely what happened, and on Tuesday she drove into Surfers Paradise and spent a number of hours among the many boutiques along Orchid Avenue, her numerous purchases merely capping a pleasurable day.

Although the days were easy to fill, it was the nights that bothered her, for once she was in bed the dark hours seemed endless as she tossed and turned, wanting the muscular warmth of Dominic's body at her side, craving release from an all-consuming need that only he could assuage.

When he telephoned unexpectedly that evening she had to force her voice to project spontaneous animation. If Dominic detected things were not as she pretended, he gave no sign, and merely confined their conversation to individual happenings over the past few days, which hurt her immeasurably, for it appeared doubtful that he missed her at all.

On Wednesday Sachi visited Marina Mirage, an extremely upmarket shopping complex fronting the broadwater on the Spit, completed a few purchases that particularly took her eye, then elected to eat lunch outdoors beneath an umbrella-shaded table. On the way back to Bayview Harbour she stopped at a video rental store and selected several movies as an alternative to programmed television, then picked up takeaway Chinese for dinner and spent a pleasurable, if lonely, evening.

Consequently she slept late the next morning, and on rising she enjoyed a breakfast of fresh fruit and cereal out on the patio while scanning the daily newspapers without any real concentration.

If she didn't do something constructive, she'd go mad, she decided scant minutes later. Yet shopping held no interest at all, and besides, she had sufficient clothes and accessories to last her a lifetime.

Perhaps she could visit one of the other theme parks? Or embark on a pleasure cruise of the canals? There were numerous organised tours, and with determination she looked up the appropriate section in the telephone directory, ascertained departure time and made a booking.

By Friday evening Sachi was an emotional wreck and unable to settle to anything. The solitude she had striven for became an enemy, for it allowed her too much time in which to think.

Twice during the day she had picked up the phone and dialled the number of Dominic's office, only to replace the receiver before the call could connect. Her appetite had disappeared completely and she only picked at food, preferring fruit and salad to anything more substantial.

At seven o'clock she could stand it no longer, and she crossed to the phone to punch out the required numbers for the Hamilton residence.

Even as she waited for the call to engage she experienced a feeling of trepidation. What if Dominic wasn't home? She closed her eyes in silent supplication. Oh, God, where was he? Surely he should have picked up the receiver by now.

Her mind raced with numerous reasons why he had not. Perhaps he was in the sauna; or maybe Brent had come down for the weekend and they had gone out for dinner. They could be playing tennis, or in the pool. Or he could have accepted a social invitation, and be at any of a number of restaurants.

'Preston.'

For a moment she thought she had imagined the sound of his voice, and it took a few seconds for it to register that he had picked up the phone.

'Dominic. It's Sachi,' she added as an afterthought, then cursed herself for being so foolish. Of course he knew who it was! 'Where were you?' Now she really did sound like a suspicious wife!

'In the shower.'

Even at a distance he sounded amused, and she felt cross with herself for not attempting to assume a bright, seemingly careless façade.

'I stayed back at the office,' he drawled in explanation, 'and only reached home fifteen minutes ago.'

All she could think of to say was a rather breathless, 'Oh.'

'Is there any particular reason why you rang?'

Sachi tightened her grip on the receiver, and wondered if she had sufficient courage to tell him she wanted to come home. 'Have you had dinner?' Coward, a tiny voice taunted.

'Not yet. I believe Janet has prepared something I can heat in the microwave.'

How could he even begin to miss her when the house was so efficiently run? Oh, how much longer could she bear to carry on like this? Waiting, *praying* for a miracle.

She hesitated, then took a deep breath. 'I wondered if you'd like to come down to the Coast.'

'For dinner?'

This was turning out worse than she thought. But then surely wholehearted enthusiasm was too much to expect?

'If you've already made plans, it doesn't matter.' Except that it did, dreadfully, and if he refused she'd fall apart.

There was a brief, almost ominous silence, then his voice came down the line as a sardonic drawl. 'What plans do you imagine I might have made, Sachi?'

'Oh, something social,' she responded quickly, almost tripping over the words in an effort to conclude the conversation. 'Really, I don't mind.' She had to get off the phone before she burst into tears, and she replaced the receiver quickly, feeling physically ill.

Why had she been so foolish as to attempt to toy with fate? *Why?* Something twisted painfully deep inside her stomach, and she closed her eyes against the agony of Dominic's rejection.

The sudden unexpected peal of the telephone sounded loud in the stillness of the apartment, and Sachi stared with detached uninterest at the electronic device.

Ignoring it, she moved slowly through to the lounge and stood gazing sightlessly through the plate-glass window out over the broadwater. The sea was calm, its glistening surface dappled with reflected sunlight.

The sheer panoramic beauty of the scene before her became lost as her thoughts strayed to the few days she and Dominic had spent in the apartment after their wedding.

Her eyes filled with tears as she dwelt on the gradual awakening of her sexuality, for it was all too easy to remember his skilled touch and her own uninhibited response. Torture to imagine it meant very little to him.

How long she stood there she had no idea, except that when she stirred out of her reverie the sun had lost some of its brightness, and there was a faint greyish-blue haze shrouding the distant high-rise buildings of central Surfers' Paradise.

The slight, imperceptible sound of a key turning in the lock riveted Sachi's attention, and she moved towards the hallway—only to stop, transfixed, as Dominic entered the apartment and quietly shut the door behind him.

He was all tautly controlled power, an inimical force which actually caused her to shudder. Even now—especially now, his impact was so strong, so darkly magnificent as to be almost menacing, and she stood frozen in fright, unable to utter so much as a sound.

His eyes were diamond-hard and infinitely dangerous—almost as if he were exercising tremendous self-control, and barely winning the battle.

There could be no escape as he walked towards her, and she unconsciously threw back her head, adopting a stance that was purely defensive.

'Why didn't you answer the phone?'

He sounded deceptively mild—too mild. Any second now he would pounce, and verbally tear her limb from limb.

Her eyes glittered in angry warning. 'What was the point?'

'We hadn't concluded our conversation.'

'Good heavens, I thought we had,' she said with brutal honesty.

'No,' Dominic contradicted, staring straight into her eyes. 'But we're about to.' His gaze lowered deliberately to the soft contours of her mouth, then slid to the curves of her breasts, their sensitive peaks tightening in involuntary anticipation of his touch.

Sachi hugged her arms together, hating him, herself, and most of all, her own traitorous body for possessing a will entirely beyond her control.

'Suppose you tell me precisely the reason behind your phone call.' His voice was tight and ruthless as he lifted a hand to cup her chin, tilting it so she couldn't escape from the merciless probing eyes seemingly intent on searing her very soul.

It would be so easy to break down and *say* she cared for him more than anyone or anything else in the world, but mere words failed her. And pride. The stubborn pride of a survivor had been too deeply ingrained for too many years to permit the admission of needing someone on which to lean; to share the hurt, the insecurity, and have it absolved.

'Analytical appraisal is your forte,' she offered with a dismal attempt at flippancy. 'Why not hazard a guess?'

His eyes narrowed at the convulsive movement in her throat, and his thumb slid down to idly caress the satin-smooth skin, lingering at the indentations and tracing their hollows before slipping up to settle beneath her jaw. 'Try honesty,' he suggested in a quiet voice that seemed to reach through to her very bones.

Her eyes flicked wide, then became shadowed beneath protective lowering lashes. 'I'm not sure I'm willing to take the risk.'

'What is there to lose?'

You! Sachi longed to scream, almost at breaking point.

His hands shifted to her shoulders, then slid down her back as he drew her close—so close that she could sense the powerful thud of his heartbeat, *feel* the controlled power in every muscle of his body.

In mesmerised fascination she watched as his head lowered, and a faint moan of despair emerged as his mouth brushed hers, then lingered at its edge before tracing the delicate contours in an evocative, featherlight touch that brought forth a wealth of delicious warmth.

Her lips parted like the petals of an exotic flower, unable to deny him an exploration of the moist, sweet depths he sought with such a degree of *tendresse* that when he finally lifted his head there were tears drenching the fine green-gold depths of her eyes and her mouth shook beyond the limits of her control.

'I could kill you,' Dominic told her with deadly softness as he viewed the spill of tears and their fine trickling flow down each of her cheeks, 'for being so blind.' A slight smile twisted the edges of his mouth, but there was no cynicism, no mockery apparent.

Sachi's heart stopped, she was willing to swear it, and her voice seemed locked into an agonising silence. She closed her eyes, afraid even to hope.

'Look at me,' he bade, sliding his hands up to frame her face. 'Sachi.'

The soft command succeeded, and she gazed at him with unblinking solemnity, seeing the strength of purpose in his arresting features.

'Do you have any conception of what it cost me to let you come here alone?' His eyes darkened and assumed an immeasurable bleakness. 'There hasn't been an hour when I haven't picked up the phone, only to replace the receiver before the call could connect.' His hands tightened fractionally. 'Every night it took a tremendous effort not to drive down here to see you, rather than go home to a frighteningly empty house that meant nothing to me without you there. I haven't slept more than a few hours each night, and Janet has all but given up preparing meals to tempt my appetite.'

He kissed her, gently at first, then with an urgent passion which left them both breathless and aching for more.

Sachi looked at him, dazed, and melted into a thousand pieces at the warmth of his smile.

'Each time we made love I was convinced you must know the extent of my emotional involvement. Yet come daylight you erected barriers, and I had to restrain myself from shaking sense into you.' He drew a deep breath, then released it slowly. 'It didn't help to discover I was deeply jealous of my own brother. He made you laugh, and it was obvious you were infinitely more relaxed in his company than you were in mine.'

For a number of heart-stopping seconds she just looked at him, unable to comprehend that there had ever been a time when he was consumed by jealousy or doubts. He was too incredibly self-assured, too much in control to suffer such precarious emotions.

'Brent is——' she faltered shakily '—someone I regard as a very dear friend—part of the family.'

She looked at him carefully, seeing the latent fire emerging from his eyes, and something else she dared not attempt to define.

Perhaps confession was good for the soul, for now that she'd started she couldn't stop.

'I wanted to hate you for making marriage the only alternative. You were so—damnably compelling,' she offered. 'An impossible force I had little hope of competing against.' She faltered, feeling helpless even now to explain. 'I imagined revenge was your ultimate motivation—a desire for a reversal of power from the days when you were my father's employee.' She lifted a hand, then let it fall down to her side, unsure, even now.

A slight shiver feathered its way over her skin as she remembered her sister's invective and hysteric behaviour. 'Simone——'

'Spent an entire summer nurturing an infatuation for me,' Dominic interrupted wryly. 'She followed my every move, managing by sheer perseverance to manoeuvre me into a few foolish situations.'

'I caught the two of you kissing in the garden shed,' Sachi owned tremulously, loath even now to admit just how badly she had been hurt by the discovery all those years ago.

'Little fool,' Dominic said huskily. 'There's a vast difference between kissing and being kissed. If you'd walked in just thirty seconds sooner, you would have seen that it was Simone who initiated the kissing.'

His eyes softened until she could almost have drowned in them. 'I love you. *Love*,' he repeated, giving her a slight shake.

A wondrous feeling of pure joy slowly unfurled until it encompassed her whole body and radiated from the depths of her beautiful eyes that changed from shadowed green to glorious gold. 'You do?'

His smile was incredibly intimate, promising so much that she found it almost impossible to breathe. 'You're my life,' he vowed gently. 'The central core around which everything revolves.' He pulled her close, so close she couldn't fail to be aware of the force of his arousal. 'I admire your fierce independence, your integrity. The way you challenge me, my motives.'

He bent his head to savour the rapidly beating pulse at the base of her throat, then traced a sensitive path to her vulnerable earlobe, nuzzling it gently, his breath teasing the stray tendrils of her hair. 'As a child you were my forbidden obsession. Now you're incredibly sensual, so generous and giving, I feel almost afraid. I want to guard you every minute of the day, protect you in such a way that no man would dare look at you, let alone touch you.' He lifted his head to look at her, his eyes deeply serious. 'Does that frighten you?'

Her eyes clung to his, and the air between them seemed suddenly charged with emotion. For a moment she was unable to speak, and her heart gave a lurch as she saw a muscle tense along his jaw.

'No.' Tears pricked the back of her eyes, and she blinked rapidly to disperse them.

'It should.' There was a brooding quality evident, an uncertainty she found unbearable, and she touched a finger to his lips.

'When you love, totally, that's how it is,' Sachi ventured simply. Unbidden, she traced the firm contours of his mouth, and felt them tremble beneath her tactile exploration. A shaft of exquisite pleasure exploded deep within her, radiating through every nerve until she felt incredibly alive. To imagine she held any power over Dominic was a heady experience, yet one she felt loath to take undue advantage of.

Sachi doubted she would ever see him so achingly vulnerable again, and her heart melted. 'I love you.' The haunting vow emerged as little more than a whisper, poignant and utterly sincere. 'More than mere words can ever convey.'

A long, shuddering sigh shook his powerful frame, and his mouth possessed hers with such hunger that she exulted in his passion as she matched it, her hands exploring the tense muscles, hating the restriction of clothing that separated the touch of her skin on his.

With slow sure movements she reached for the buttons on his shirt, seeking the firm springy hair whorling his chest, then stood utterly still as he reciprocated, discarding first her blouse, then her bra, freeing the sensitised flesh of her breasts to his gaze.

'You're beautiful, Sachi. So incredibly exquisite.' He caressed one taut roseate peak, then made a similar supplication to its twin before lifting her up against him.

She cried out as his tongue savoured her breast, drawing it gently between his teeth to render such delicious torture that she slid her fingers through his hair to urge his head away, silently begging him

to shift his attention and ease the almost unbearable ecstasy spiralling through her body.

Unbidden, she arched against him, unconscious
of the tiny almost guttural sounds that left her lips
in a husky plea, and Dominic groaned as he relinquished his mouth.

'Witch,' he muttered with a wry musing smile.
'I can't keep my hands off you!'

A slow tide of colour crept over Sachi's cheeks
as she saw the naked ardour in his gaze, and knew
her own eyes were slumbrous with answering
passion.

'Perhaps we should do something about dinner,'
she considered with a mischievous smile. 'We could
celebrate with candelight and champagne in some
exclusive restaurant.'

A finger trailed the outline of her mouth, then
slid down her throat to the valley between her
breasts.

'It's still daylight,' she protested, unable to resist
teasing him a little. 'And a confession of love de-
serves a very special celebration.'

The expression in his eyes kindled, then settled
into something resembling musing resignation as
she threaded her fingers through his and led the
way down the hallway.

In the bedroom she crossed to the windows and
released each sash containing the heavy curtains so
the edges fell, then met together, successfully closing
out the world.

Slowly she turned towards him and began to
remove each remaining garment with care before
taking the necessary few steps to bring her within
touching distance.

Inside she was trembling as her fingers reached for the belt of his trousers and freed the clasp, and there was no way to control their shaky attempt with the zip fastening.

A hand covered both her own, while the other took hold of her chin and lifted it high.

'My darling Sachi,' Dominic warned with a husky growl, 'as much as I'd delight in having you unclothe me, I should advise you *now* that there's a limit to my control. If you want to get out of this apartment at all, I suggest you call a halt.'

Her mouth shook as she attempted a smile. 'But I haven't really begun.'

His eyes flared, and the tiny lines fanning out towards each temple seemed to deepen as he uttered a subdued deep-throated laugh. 'I can't think of any valid reason for you to stop.'

'Not even the fact that I've never attempted to seduce a man before?'

He lowered his head and kissed her with such gentle evocativeness that she almost cried.

'If you need help,' he promised softly, 'I'll guide you.'

'You've always taken great care to pleasure me,' she began on a tremulous note. With shaky fingers she slowly divested him of every article of clothing. It was crazy to feel so nervous, yet she did, wondering even as she lightly began to trace the musculature of his ribcage if she could carry her intentions to their ultimate conclusion.

'Do you imagine for one minute that *I* didn't derive complete satisfaction from your response?'

His eyes were darker than she had ever seen them appear before, and there was such a wealth of tenderness apparent, it wiped out any last vestige of doubt.

'I want to give you a total satiation of the senses,' Sachi said a trifle unsteadily. 'With all my love.'

A long time afterwards, as she lay entwined in his arms, she retained no clear memory of when his possession had taken control over hers. She only knew the long, slow loving transcended anything they had previously shared, and she felt at peace. All the doubts, the uncertainty and the pain were wiped out as if they never existed.

The moon spilled a silvery luminescence, lighting several rooms in the apartment with long-reaching shadowy fingers, and Sachi sighed, a slight, breathy sound that mirrored utter contentment.

Dominic stirred, and his arm tightened fractionally as he brushed his lips against her temple. 'Thank you,' he said gently, and a light blush coloured her cheeks.

Their shared delight in each other had vaguely shocked her, yet she felt no shame, just a glorious sense of physical and mental attunement.

'No more doubts?' he queried, and a soft smile curved her lips as she shook her head.

'None.'

He kissed her hard, wreaking a devastating assault that plundered her senses and left her clinging to him in unrestrained abandon.

When he finally lifted his head she almost died at the wealth of passion evident, a deep, abiding desire that promised ecstasy.

'I guess we don't get to eat dinner,' Sachi voiced without an ounce of regret, and his eyes gleamed with hidden laughter.

'Indeed we do. Later.'

PENNY JORDAN

Sins and infidelities...
Dreams and obsessions...
Shattering secrets
unfold in...

THE HIDDEN YEARS

SAGE — stunning, sensual and vibrant, she spent a lifetime distancing herself from a past too painful to confront... the mother who seemed to hold her at bay, the father who resented her and the heartache of unfulfilled love. To the world, Sage was independent and invulnerable— but it was a mask she cultivated to hide a desperation she herself couldn't quite understand... until an unforeseen turn of events drew her into the discovery of the hidden years, finally allowing Sage to open her heart to a passion denied for so long.

The Hidden Years—a compelling novel of truth and passion that will unlock the heart and soul of every woman.

AVAILABLE IN OCTOBER!
Watch for your opportunity to complete your Penny Jordan set.
POWER PLAY and SILVER will also be available in October.

HIDDEN

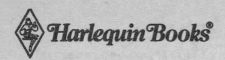 **Harlequin Books®**

GREAT NEWS...
HARLEQUIN UNVEILS NEW SHIPPING PLANS

For the convenience of customers, Harlequin has announced that Harlequin romances will now be available in stores at these convenient times each month*:

Harlequin Presents, American Romance, Historical, Intrigue:

> May titles: April 10
> June titles: May 8
> July titles: June 5
> August titles: July 10

Harlequin Romance, Superromance, Temptation, Regency Romance:

> May titles: April 24
> June titles: May 22
> July titles: June 19
> August titles: July 24

We hope this new schedule is convenient for you.

With only two trips each month to your local bookseller, you'll never miss any of your favorite authors!

*Please note: There may be slight variations in on-sale dates in your area due to differences in shipping and handling.
*Applicable to U.S. only.

HDATES-RR

Harlequin Superromance®

Available in Superromance this month
#462—STARLIT PROMISE

STARLIT PROMISE is a deeply moving story of a
woman coming to terms with her grief and gradually
opening her heart to life and love.

Author Petra Holland sets the scene beautifully, never
allowing her heroine to become mired in self-pity. It
is a story that will touch your heart and leave you
celebrating the strength of the human spirit.

Available wherever Harlequin books
are sold.

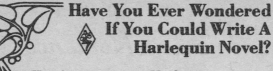

Have You Ever Wondered If You Could Write A Harlequin Novel?

Here's great news—Harlequin is offering a series of cassette tapes to help you do just that. Written by Harlequin editors, these tapes give practical advice on how to make your characters—and your story—come alive. There's a tape for each contemporary romance series Harlequin publishes.

Mail order only

All sales final

--------------------------------✂----------------------------------

Clip this coupon and return to:

H A R L E Q U I N
American Romance®

From the Alaskan wilderness to sultry New Orleans...from New England seashores to the rugged Rockies...American Romance brings you the best of America. And with each trip, you'll find the best in romance.

Each month, American Romance brings you the magic of falling in love with that special American man. Whether an untamed cowboy or a polished executive, he has that sensuality, that special spark sure to capture your heart.

For stories of today, with women just like you and the men they dream about, read American Romance. Four new titles each month.

HARLEQUIN AMERICAN ROMANCE—the love stories you can believe in.

AMERICAN